BITE ME (I LOVE YOU)

VANESSA NORTH

"[A]uthentic characters charting complicated paths with grace and courage."

The New York Times on BLUEBERRY BOYS

"A beautiful look at female relationships."

The Washington Post on ROLLER GIRL

"A steamy book in which nuanced friendships are as central as the romance between two star-crossed lovers."

Kirkus on SUMMER STOCK

"Steamy and compelling"

RT Book Reviews on DOUBLE UP

"Smooth and sexy"

Publisher's Weekly on ROUGH ROAD

"[A] fabulous romance with two male leads."

RT Book Reviews on SUMMER STOCK

Chapter One

AS FAR AS JOBS WENT, looking at Tommy Nguyen's perfect face all day was not a difficult one. The host of *Science Sunday* was charming and handsome, effortlessly engaging. On screen, he was riveting. Too bad his secrets were an inconvenient pain in Felix's ass.

"Cut." The director's order echoed through the set and Felix stopped his camera. "Take a break, everyone."

The set, located in a nondescript office building in Atlanta's midtown, was warm and they'd been taping all day. Felix gestured to the lighting operator to cut the set lights.

Tommy stretched sinuously, and Felix tried not to stare as the man's T-shirt rode up and exposed a flat stretch of smooth skin. He liked looking at Tommy, but staring without the camera between them was a bad idea.

They'd been working together for five years, and Tommy had never intentionally given Felix any indication that he was interested in other men. He was so far in the closet, he probably had tea with Mr. Tumnus.

Felix knew because he paid attention to Tommy.

Working for a news network meant that they heard about breaking stories before the public did. And whenever there was a mass shooting about to hit the news, Tommy stopped whatever he was doing and called a friend. The person Tommy called was a man named Alden Kaufman who had survived a mass shooting in North Carolina several years earlier. Felix had heard enough of those conversations to know that they were careful, concerned, and loving in a painfully-thwarted-romance way.

Felix also knew that Tommy took occasional trips to the North Carolina mountains because he had a friends with benefits arrangement with an ex. He didn't make a secret of that, though he probably worded it more politely. Alden Kaufman lived outside of Asheville. It wasn't hard to put two and two together.

So, Felix knew, but he couldn't look at Tommy like he wanted to, because he wouldn't look at a straight guy like that. And he wasn't supposed to know Tommy wasn't straight.

And now, they had to have a conversation that was made all that much harder because it would be so much easier if Felix didn't have to pretend that he didn't know who Tommy was going to visit in North Carolina.

"Hey, Nguyen," he called out, and Tommy looked up at him, meeting his gaze. A hint of a smile flickered around his lips and it made something careen around in Felix's guts. Off screen, Tommy's smiles were rare. Felix was painfully aware how few people on the set could earn those smiles, and equally painfully aware that Tommy *always* smiled when Felix said his name.

"What's up, Pearce?" Tommy made his way over.

"The studio sent over my flight reservations for the Maine trip. Any idea why I've got a two-day layover in Asheville, North Carolina?"

Tommy's face blanched slightly, but to anyone else he wouldn't have seemed to react at all to Felix's question. "I didn't make your reservations, Pearce. Why don't you ask the travel desk?"

"Just wondering if maybe we were on the same flights?" Felix and Tommy were like salt and pepper shakers as far as the travel desk was concerned. Always a pair. Always together. Even when they contracted with other crews on location, Felix went with Tommy. No one knew Tommy better, and for some reason, Tommy seemed to like him. Felix was very aware that Tommy didn't like a lot of people. Even with the people he did like, he didn't let his affections show often—not *really*. But Felix had spent the last five years watching Tommy Nguyen through his lens, and he could read him like his favorite dog-eared sci fi novel.

Tommy shrugged, then gave Felix a genuine smile. "Okay, you got me. It's my fault. Since we had a few days before our equipment would arrive in Maine, I wanted to visit my friend in Asheville. I guess the travel desk assumed we would travel together. Did they book you a hotel room at least?"

Felix sighed. "No, they didn't. I'll get them to change my flights."

Easier said than done. It turned out the studio, always so budget-minded, had booked a non-refundable flight, and it was going to cost more to change it than to put him up in a hotel room for two nights.

"I've heard Asheville is nice," the girl on the phone chirped apologetically.

Felix grunted. "Just put me somewhere I can walk places. I don't want to bother with a rental car."

"You've got it. I'll email you your reservation information in just a few minutes. Can I do anything else for you today?"

"No, thank you." God knew they'd done enough. He returned to the set to find Tommy back on his mark, reading glasses perched on his nose, going over the final segment with the director. Tommy didn't work from a script, but he did write out notes beforehand. He had a knack for distilling science concepts down to language small kids could understand and relate to. And then he showed how the concepts applied in the world around them. Felix had learned more about science as Tommy's cameraman than he had in school.

Tommy glanced up at him. "Did you get it sorted?"

Felix shook his head. "Looks like I'm spending two days in Asheville."

"I'm sorry." And he looked like he actually meant it before he gave Felix an impish smile. "But I'm glad I'll have someone to talk to on the plane."

Felix blew out a breath and smiled. "You know, you could read a book."

Tommy nodded. "Yes, I could. But I enjoy listening to you talk about the ones you're reading."

And then they went back to work, and Felix wasn't annoyed anymore because Tommy preferred his company to books, and wasn't that something?

TOMMY WAVED goodbye to Felix at the Asheville airport. He felt bad about accidentally stranding the other man in a strange city for two days, but the short flight from Atlanta had been fun. Felix Pearce had a way of keeping conversations going and avoiding awkward silences that Tommy admired and appreciated. A few times, Tommy had been tempted to tell Felix the truth about his Asheville visits. Felix seemed like the type who could keep a secret. But no, what was the expression? Two can keep a secret if one of them is dead? And the risks were just too high. It was hard enough being an Asian man on TV. To be a *gay* Asian man on TV? Hosting a children's show? He didn't want the trouble.

Thank God he had Alden.

In the Uber from the airport to Alden's house, Tommy let himself begin to fantasize about how he would spend the next two days, hopefully mostly in bed. Alden was a bossy, demanding lover, and also Tommy's best friend in the world. He knew exactly what Tommy liked and had a penchant for dirty talk that could curl a man's toes. And when Tommy left in two days, he'd be deeply satisfied physically, and reassured that his reclusive ex-boyfriend was okay emotionally.

It was the most he could hope for these days. Between his traveling for the show and the firmly closed closet door, he had no opportunity to find a bedmate he could trust. Alden was safe, and he never turned Tommy away. It would be good—for both of them—and if he sometimes wished they had the kind of relationship they'd had before Alden had been shot in the food court of a shopping mall, well, that was just nostalgia. Everyone got nostalgic now and again.

The Uber dropped him off in front of a small bungalow in the suburbs. It had a ramp installed by the front steps for Alden's mother's wheelchair, and the ground was carpeted by orange leaves that had fallen from the large maple tree towering over the house. It was a place that held years of memories for Tommy, and he grinned as he climbed the steps, his backpack over his shoulder.

He knocked on Alden's door more out of custom than

because he expected an answer. A shivery rush of anticipation ran through him as he pulled out his phone and sent a text.

Tommy: You there man? I'm on your front steps.

A few minutes later, the door swung open, and there he was. Tommy's first—and only—love. Alden Kaufman was slender and blond with icy, blue-gray eyes. Beautiful, brilliant, and so, so broken. Regret clamped down on Tommy's heart, but he pushed it back.

"Hi," Alden said quietly. There was something different about him. Tommy couldn't quite put his finger on it but Alden seemed comfortable—even serene. Maybe he'd tried some new therapy or something. He looked more content than Tommy had seen him in years.

"Hey, Al. You look good." *Too good.* The hairs raised on the back of Tommy's neck, because he suddenly had the sense that he didn't belong here anymore. But that was ridiculous, wasn't it? To hide his sudden nerves, Tommy ran a hand through his hair and then pulled Alden into a hug.

Alden relaxed into the embrace, holding Tommy tight against him for a moment. Tommy breathed in the smell of Alden and squeezed his shoulders, his dick plumping up in a pavlovian response. Before he could lean in and kiss Alden, his friend stepped away and held open the door.

"Come on in."

Tommy stepped into the house and reached for his cigarettes. Alden never minded Tommy smoking in his house, which Tommy really fucking appreciated because his one vice made it possible for him to relax when Alden was being weird. And Alden was always weird. Except he wasn't being weird, which meant *Tommy* was.

"I can make coffee," Alden said, leading Tommy into the kitchen. "How long are you in town for?"

"Two days, give or take. Can I crash here?" This conversation always went the same, and Alden would recognize the question as what it really was: *Will you let me into your bed again, because I don't have anyone else and I need to touch someone so much?*

Alden set down the can of coffee abruptly and stared at the floor. "I, um… I don't think it's a good idea."

What the hell?

Tommy glanced around the familiar kitchen, taking in a few subtle changes. There was a laptop on the table. A giant jacket hanging on the hook. A pair of running shoes —sitting next to Alden's and much, much larger— cemented Tommy's growing suspicion.

"Oh shit. You're with someone. You're—you're living with someone?"

How the hell had that happened? Alden was agoraphobic and didn't go *out* like that—as far as Tommy knew, he hadn't been on so much as a date since their breakup *years* ago. He steeled his face not to show his surprise. If Alden was with someone, that was good—wasn't it?

"No." Alden shook his head. "At least not like that. He's just a friend. And he had knee surgery…"

Alden trailed off, and it was clear from the expression on his face he didn't believe a word he was saying. Alden *was* with someone. And it was still new.

"Liar." Tommy teased. "Nothing about the look on your face says 'just a friend.'" He lit his cigarette and grinned at Alden. He brutally shoved away his disappointment at this turn of events. So, maybe he wasn't going to get laid this weekend. Alden was *happy.* Tommy hadn't been sure he'd ever see Alden happy again. He held out the pack of cigarettes to Alden, who shook his head. "What's he like?"

Alden's face lit up and he smiled. "Big. Brawny like a

lumberjack, but gentle. Thoughtful, stubborn, and ridiculously hot."

Tommy couldn't help but smile at that. Alden almost sounded offended that his new friend was hot. Good for Alden. "Nice. He isn't straight, is he? Cause if you're not hitting that…"

Alden actually giggled. Damn. Tommy had missed that laugh. "No, not straight. And I didn't say I wasn't hitting that. It's complicated. But it's not a *thing*."

Tommy felt a lump forming in his throat. Dammit. He was *not* going to get all emotional. He went to the window to cover his reaction. He opened the window and flicked his ashes outside. He tried for levity, but he wasn't sure he managed.

"I'm jealous. I want a complicated, ridiculously hot but gentle lumberjack available for middle of the night hookups. Whose dick did you suck to arrange that?"

"Mine."

Tommy turned, taking in the newcomer. Big was an understatement. The man was well over six feet tall, with curly brown hair and bulging muscles. And he was on crutches. How did someone that big manage to sneak up on people? On crutches?

The big man smiled sweetly at Alden, then turned to Tommy. "Tommy Nguyen, right? From *Science Sunday*? Alden never mentioned that he knew you. I'm Kit Taylor."

He held out his hand and Tommy took it, feeling small in every possible way as they shook hands. He smiled, but he wasn't sure it reached his eyes. "Nice to meet you, Kit Taylor. Are you a science fan?"

It was his standard icebreaker. Sure, his show was technically children's programming, but lots of adults watched it too.

"He's a field biologist." Alden answered for Kit. "We work together."

Alden turned to his "friend" and asked him a question about physical therapy. When Kit asked for a cup of the coffee, Tommy jumped at the chance to be useful. He poured the coffee with shaking hands and then dug in the fridge for cream.

He handed the cream and sugar to Kit as he joined them at the table. "I guess these are yours? Alden always takes his black."

"Kit has a sweet tooth," Alden babbled inanely. Kit and Tommy both looked at him curiously. Could this be any more awkward?

"So Tommy, Alden didn't mention you'd be visiting," Kit said. Tommy took a drag on his cigarette and leaned back in his chair.

"I didn't know I was coming until the last minute. I probably wouldn't have if I'd known—" he gestured at Alden and then Kit. "Well. That."

The temperature in the room seemed to drop ten degrees. Kit glared at Alden. "Am I cock-blocking you? Want me to go take a drive around the neighborhood? Maybe go back to my place for a couple of days?"

Oh, shit. This was bad. Whatever was going on between these two, Tommy was ninety-nine percent sure it had to do with Alden's inability to communicate effectively. Tommy couldn't be hurt by it anymore, but this new guy was practically radiating hurt feelings. Dammit, Alden.

"I'm going to finish my smoke outside." Tommy picked up the ashtray and let himself outside. He hoped Alden would be able to sort things out with Kit. They both obviously had strong feelings for each other. And Alden deserved to have something good in his life.

The voices inside raised, Kit's deep and hurt, Alden's

getting higher and more indignant as the conversation wore on. They were fighting. Then, Tommy heard the door on the other side of the house slam, and he jumped at the noise.

He took a deep breath and let himself back inside to end things—again, and forever—with the only man he'd ever loved.

Chapter Two

FELIX WAS DRESSING to go out when his phone buzzed. He picked it up and looked at the text message.

Tommy: It seems my ex has gone and fallen in love, so I'm going to need to find a hotel room for the night. Where are you staying?

Felix stared at the phone, bemused, then texted back the name of the hotel. The whole reason they were stuck in Asheville for the weekend was so Tommy could get laid and he hadn't even bothered to check to see if his ex was still single?

Felix: I was about to go grab lunch. Want me to wait for you?

Tommy: Sure. Thanks.

Felix: I'm in room 1412. Meet me here after you get checked in.

Felix lay back on the bed and stared at the ceiling. The hotel was a nice one, with a conference center and spa attached. The lobby had been crowded when he'd arrived, but the rooms were clean and quiet. They were decorated in that bland, modern way so many hotels were these days. White linens and dark wood, mirrors everywhere. A pleasant place to spend a few days.

He'd considered looking on his favorite hookup apps to

see if he could arrange a date—why should Tommy be the only one getting laid? But now he was wondering what had happened with Tommy's ex and was spinning out the fantasy of Tommy getting over the ex by getting under Felix.

Tommy would be wild between the sheets. Felix wasn't sure how he knew, but there was a spark of something every time he looked at Tommy—and he spent a lot of time looking at Tommy—that made him absolutely certain he'd be incredible in bed.

Maybe it was time to let on that he knew Tommy's secret. And what happened in Asheville could stay in Asheville. He was hard now, just from thinking about Tommy. All these years he hadn't let himself indulge these fantasies, but now—hell. *Now.* He ran a hand down his chest, skimming over a nipple and feeling a surge of lust. He palmed himself through his jeans, then let go and sighed.

Yeah, he could jerk himself off and that would be fun, but then he'd have to share a lunch table with the man he'd been thinking about and that was just awkward.

He pulled open the books app on his phone and began to read the thriller he'd started on the plane: a revenge fantasy about a woman getting even with the men who'd done her wrong. He got so absorbed in the story, he was startled when he heard a knock on his door. He set the phone down and crossed to the door, looking through the peephole to confirm it was Tommy collecting him for lunch. He swung the door open.

"Hey. Ready for lun—Why do you have your luggage?"

Tommy scowled. "So, this is awkward, but, there's some kind of machinists convention happening, and a wedding, and something else, and they're so sorry, but they don't have any rooms. Can I please crash in here with you?"

Felix swallowed and stepped back and waved Tommy into the room. The truth was going to have to come out now. Otherwise Tommy would be cagey and weird. "Sure but—there's only one bed."

Tommy dropped his pack to the floor, swore, then stared up at the ceiling as if he were lecturing God. Finally he looked back at Felix. "Well, this is getting even more awkward."

"It doesn't have to be. I've slept in closer quarters. Come on, get settled in and we'll go grab lunch."

Tommy looked around the room, tension in his shoulders, which he then shrugged off and moved his bag over to the desk. Then he sat down in the chair next to it and buried his face in his hands. Felix wasn't sure what to say. The man clearly had feelings for his ex that went beyond friendship with benefits. Ah, hell. They were going to have to talk about it.

"Come on, let's go get lunch. I'll buy you a drink and you can tell me all about it."

They chose a restaurant a quick walk from the hotel. The fall air was crisp and cool, and Felix pulled his jacket tightly around his body. At first, they didn't speak, so Felix broke the ice.

"So, your ex has a new man?"

Tommy sighed and looked at him. "Yeah. I guess all good things come to an end."

"You didn't even think to check to see if he was single before flying us up here for a booty call?"

"Trust me, it's *incredibly* unexpected. Wait—Dammit, Pearce."

Felix smiled at that.

"How long have you known?" Tommy asked, staring

ahead, world-weary. "And how? Does everyone at work know?"

"A couple years. I'm observant. And no, I don't think anyone else knows. You play your cards very close to your chest."

"Please don't tell anyone."

It was Felix's turn to scowl. "Dude, I wouldn't out you. I'm not an asshole. Is this it?" He gestured as they arrived at the restaurant.

"Yeah." Tommy opened the door and held it for him.

"Thanks."

They were seated immediately, and they both ordered beer, then studied the menu. It was typical gastro-pub fare. Burgers and sandwiches, fancy appetizers and salads. After they ordered—sandwiches for both of them—they sat in silence for a long moment.

"I'm gay," Felix said. "So, you know. I get it. We work on a kids' show, et cetera. I'm not judging you."

Tommy stared at him for a moment, then nodded thoughtfully and played with his fork. "I never would have guessed. I guess you're more observant than I am."

Felix shrugged. "I look at you through a camera for a living. I've spent more time observing you."

"That's actually a little creepy, Pearce." Tommy laughed. "But, point taken."

"Your ex was in that shooting, wasn't he?"

"Yes. When we were still together. It was a contributing factor in our breakup. And I know that makes me a shitty person."

Felix shook his head. "No, it doesn't. It's not like you broke up with him because he got shot, is it?"

Tommy shook his head. "No. In hindsight, I could have handled everything better. I didn't really know how to be a good boyfriend to a guy with PTSD. But that's not why."

Their sandwiches arrived and they ate in silence for a few minutes before Felix struck up the conversation again.

"So this breakup today—the end of the hookup era—it's been a long time coming."

That got a smile out of Tommy. "I guess so. But it's hard to see the only person you've ever loved head over heels for someone else. Don't get me wrong—I'm so glad he's happy. I really am. I just wish—I wish he could have been happy with me."

"So why did you really break up the first time?"

"Because I was working on development for *Science Sunday*, and he was a fucking mess after the shooting, and we were fighting all the time. When the show got the green light, that was it. I left, and I didn't invite him to come with me."

"No offense, but it doesn't sound like a great love affair."

"I did love him." Tommy insisted. "I loved him in the way you love someone when you're young and you smell possibilities everywhere. He was clever and beautiful and it was impossible not to love him. But he changed, and so did what he wanted from me."

Felix scoffed. "That's not love. It's infatuation. If it were love, you couldn't fuck him and leave him over and over again. For *years.* Do you really think you'd be content with two days here and there if you loved each other?"

Tommy scowled. "I was given an opportunity to be on TV. And that meant there was no room in my life for clever boys who smell like possibilities."

Shaking his head, Felix laughed. "Come on, man. If you loved him, you wouldn't give him up for TV. You'd make room in your life for all his possibilities."

Tommy's face took on that cool, cynical mask he wore off camera. "Says the guy who lives like a monk. I've known you five years and had no idea you were gay. When was the last time *you* got laid?"

Felix wasn't going to let Tommy turn this around on him. Sparring verbally with Tommy could be fun, but this conversation was veering into interesting territory. "I can get laid any time I want, Nguyen."

Tommy smirked. "In other words, it's been so long you don't remember."

"I remember. And I guarantee he does too. When I fuck, I leave marks."

Tommy's mouth dropped open and his eyes widened. Then he shivered and took a long drink of his beer. "Well. That's certainly a thing to say."

Felix laughed.

"I don't even know how to respond to that." Tommy continued. "Jesus, Pearce."

"Sorry, I couldn't help myself." Felix was most definitely *not* sorry. "You should have seen your face."

Tommy raised one sardonic eyebrow. "I'm sure. You know, it takes a lot to surprise me, and I've had a quite a few today. Can we talk about something—anything—that isn't my sex life or yours?"

Felix picked up his sandwich again and grinned. "Sure, what do you want to talk about?"

WHEN I FUCK, *I leave marks.* Felix's words rattled around in Tommy's head as they walked back to the hotel, and he didn't realize he was holding his breath until black spots appeared in front of his eyes. He let out the breath and reached for his cigarettes. A smoke would settle his nerves.

"Do you mind?" he asked, though he really didn't care if Felix minded. He was only asking to be polite.

"Go ahead."

Tommy lit the cigarette and took a deep inhale, then blew the smoke away from his companion. "So. We all know what my plans for the evening were. What were you going to do?"

"Well, I *was* thinking about getting some strange."

Tommy nearly coughed but caught himself. "Great, now I'm cock-blocking you too?"

Felix smiled, a very nice, warm smile, as he glanced over at Tommy. "It's fine."

Tommy studied Felix as surreptitiously as possible. The two of them had traveled all over the country together. He knew the lines of Felix's body and face as well as he knew anyone in the world. Felix Pearce had wide shoulders, bulky from carrying equipment. Lean legs and long arms. Brown eyes with crinkles at the corners. From the perfect cut of his light brown hair—the hair of a man who visited a barber regularly—to the soles of his sensible hiking shoes, Felix was familiar to Tommy. But this revelation that he was gay, and that apparently he liked the kind of sex that left marks? That was a side of him that was wholly unfamiliar. And Tommy was curious. Who wouldn't be?

This man he thought he knew—this man who was his colleague, his companion, his friend—had suddenly blind-sided Tommy.

He could see now how the night would unfold. Sharing a hotel bed, holding his breath at every accidental touch. *Marks.* Every movement, every sigh, every snore or roll would catch his attention. *When I fuck, I leave marks.* And every inch of Tommy would burn. It would be torture. But how could he back out now?

He hadn't finished his cigarette when they arrived back

at the hotel, so he stayed outside to finish it, expecting Felix would go ahead to the room without him. But instead, Felix stood in the cold and waited, as if keeping Tommy company was important to him. And what if it was? What if Felix's revelation was also an admission? What if he was burning too?

Awareness crackled in the air between them.

"What kind of marks?" Tommy finally asked.

A slow smile spread across Felix's face. He reached out and took the cigarette from Tommy's hand, then took a drag from it and extinguished it. How on earth could the man make putting a cigarette out look sexy?

"Come on." Felix gestured toward the door. "Let's have this conversation in private."

They rode the elevator to the fourteenth floor in silence. Tommy was aware of Felix's body heat next to him, and of his own arousal. His skin felt tight and hot, and his dick was hard in his jeans. *Marks.*

Felix opened the door to the room and let Tommy enter first.

"I don't—" Tommy began as the door swung shut, but Felix stopped him with a finger on his lips.

"Let me say something first."

Tommy swallowed and nodded.

"We work together. And I like our working relationship. I don't want to do anything that would jeopardize that."

Tommy drew in a deep breath and nodded. This was Felix letting him down easy. Fair enough. "I don't either."

"That said—we're alone in a strange city. We can make our own rules for what we want this to be. Blowing off a little steam? Killing time? I'm fine with that."

Oh. Felix wasn't rejecting him—he was negotiating.

"I can't stop thinking about what you said. What kind of marks?"

"Come here." Felix drew him close and slowly, carefully lowered his head and captured Tommy's lips in a kiss.

It was gentle, far more so than Tommy expected. Lips finding a fit, hands reaching for closeness. And then it wasn't gentle at all. Tommy's lips parted, Felix's tongue swept in, and they were both hard and frantic, pushing at each other and grasping for leverage. Felix propelled them through the room to the bed and pushed Tommy down onto it. They kissed and rolled, all thrusting hips and heat between them. Then Felix was on top, kissing along Tommy's jaw, nipping at his ear, and rocking his hips into the cradle of Tommy's thighs.

"Fuck." Tommy swore and dropped his head back. "What kind of marks, Pearce?"

"Can I take your shirt off?" Felix asked.

Tommy nodded. "If you take yours off too."

Not fast enough for either of them, Felix stripped out of his shirt and threw it on the floor, then yanked Tommy's over his head and tossed it over his shoulder to join it.

"I like kissing." Felix ran a hand over Tommy's chest. "And biting. And scratching." He scraped his nails across Tommy's belly gently. "I don't have to leave marks, but I'd like to see them on your skin."

A jolt of lust shot through Tommy. "That sounds fucking hot."

Felix smiled. "Yeah, well, you know I think it is. But if I do something you don't like or aren't into, stop me, okay? And I won't leave anything that will show on camera."

Then he kissed his way down Tommy's chest, biting and sucking red marks onto Tommy's skin. He teased a nipple between two fingers then scratched Tommy's abs again. Tommy closed his eyes and raised his arms over his head, letting out a low moan.

"Is this okay?" Felix asked.

"Yeah, Pearce. It feels good." Tommy smiled without opening his eyes.

A harder scratch down his side made Tommy shudder.

"Call me Felix."

Tommy opened his eyes and looked down to meet Felix's gaze. "Felix," he agreed. "What you're doing feels good. Do more."

Felix grinned and bit Tommy right above his navel. It was a quick, sharp nip that curled Tommy's toes.

"Can I take your jeans and underwear off?"

"Hell yes." Tommy breathed the words more than said them. He'd never had a bed partner ask permission like that, and the way it filled him with anticipation was intoxicating.

He closed his eyes while Felix stripped the rest of his clothes from him. Where would Felix touch him next?

A bite to his instep. A scratch down his thigh. A nibble at his kneecap. A luxurious heat built in Tommy's body as Felix explored. His skin became more sensitive than it had ever been as he relaxed under the caring cruelty of Felix's mouth and fingernails. A part of him wanted to cry, it felt so good to have this man's attention on him, these touches that weren't like the kind of sex Tommy was used to but were so much more focused, and all on him, all *for* him.

His hips pulsed up, and he reached for his cock. Felix stopped his hand, pressing a kiss to his palm that turned into a bite. "Not yet," he whispered.

Tommy opened his eyes. "You're killing me."

Felix licked over Tommy's hipbone, then bit down, sending more sparks of arousal through Tommy. "No, I think I'll eat you alive."

He moved back up Tommy's body and kissed him deeply, making a rough noise in his throat and grabbing Tommy's jaw in one big hand. Tommy thrust up against him, his cock catching on the rough denim of Felix's jeans. He groaned into Felix's mouth.

"Will you take your clothes off too?" He rocked up into Felix again.

Felix nipped at his earlobe and scissored it lightly between his teeth. "Okay," he said.

Tommy pushed himself up onto his elbows to watch as Felix stripped his jeans off, then a pair of black boxer briefs. Good lord. Who knew his cameraman had all *that* for equipment. His mouth watered. Felix had a thick cock and heavy, pendulous balls. He looked *delicious.* He gave himself a single stroke and then grinned at Tommy.

"The way you're looking at me—do you have *any* idea how good it feels to be looked at like that? You look hungry."

Did he? Well, of course he did.

"Can I suck you?" Tommy asked.

Felix shook his head. "Not yet." He joined Tommy on the bed again, and they started kissing like that was the main event. Who knew maybe for Felix it was? He was *really* into it, running his hands through Tommy's short hair and scraping his fingernails on Tommy's scalp, nipping at lips and chin and neck.

Did he enjoy receiving those sensations as much as he enjoyed giving them? Tommy ran a hand over the firm muscles of Felix's chest, then made an experimental scratch of his own.

"Ohhhhh," Felix shivered. "Do *that.* Harder."

Tommy swallowed thickly and repeated the motion. "Like this?"

He watched as Felix's eyes rolled back, a growing sense of confidence building. No longer content to lie back and let Felix take the lead, he started exploring, biting and scratching and kissing just like Felix had done to him.

Except when he got below the waist, he decided to play dirty.

He took Felix's cock in one hand and lightly ran a fingernail down the shaft. Felix dragged in a sharp breath and held it. Tommy stroked him with one hand and took just the very tip into his mouth. He sucked at the salty head of Felix's cock, and Felix let out a low, lust-filled groan. Tommy hummed encouragement and dug his fingernails into Felix's thigh.

"Tommy, stop."

He stopped, looking up at Felix. Maybe receiving wasn't Felix's catnip. "Did I do something wrong?"

Felix shook his head. "No, this is—this is amazing. But if you do all that, I'm going to come. I want to make sure it's good for you first."

Well, who could argue with that?

"It's good for me." He stretched out next to Felix. "You're not what I expected."

Felix bit Tommy's chest, harder than before. "What do you mean?"

"You like to be in charge, but you're not... Well, you're not bossy."

Felix grinned and twisted Tommy's nipple. "I can be, if that's what you're into."

Tommy lay back and stretched his arms overhead. "I think I'm into whatever you want to do."

"Thank you." The grin on Felix's face widened, and he kissed Tommy again, deep and lush. Again, Tommy felt that luxuriant lassitude spreading through him, that deep relaxation that somehow was bringing tears to his eyes.

This time, when Felix's teeth closed on Tommy's shoulder, Tommy arched his back, letting the pleasure and pain wash over him together. The bite became a hard suck, the kind that would leave a bruise, just as Felix's hand closed over Tommy's cock.

Jesus. Something must be short-circuiting in Tommy's brain because he felt that sucking on his shoulder *everywhere.* It was as if Felix's mouth was on his shoulder and his dick and his nipple all together. Felix's hand was pumping him slowly and surely, and then his teeth were closing on Tommy's biceps—who knew the biceps were an erogenous zone? Tommy could do nothing but lie back and take it, the rough bites, the tender stroke of Felix's hand, a scratch across his nipple that sent him arching off the bed.

The orgasm shocked him. He'd been so relaxed, so covered in sensation that the sharp climb hit him hard and fast. Felix's teeth closed on his shoulder again, and Tommy yelled out in desperate joy. He thrust up into Felix's hand, completely abandoning any pretense at dignity as he came apart.

He felt boneless as he sank back to the bed. Felix let go of his cock and grinned down at him. "You're beautiful when you come."

Tommy flushed. He'd been told he was beautiful his whole life, but not like this. Never like this.

"Come see." Felix helped him sit up and face the mirror. "See this." He stroked a hand over Tommy's shoulder where a red bruise was forming, then down his chest to where three red scratches stood out on his skin. "This turns me on so much."

Tommy smiled at their reflections. He looked a hot mess. Spunk drying on his belly. Marks all over him. He looked well-fucked and happy. He reached up and pulled Felix into a kiss, then pushed him down on the bed. This time, when he took Felix into his mouth and began to suck, Felix moaned happily, stroking a fingertip over the bruise on Tommy's shoulder.

Tommy rolled Felix's heavy balls in one hand, and Felix began to thrust. Tommy relaxed his jaw and let Felix fuck his mouth. He could tell from the frantic, jerky movements that Felix was close.

"I'm going to come," Felix warned. "Tommy—"

Tommy shook his head and swallowed around the tip of Felix's cock. Felix cried out, throwing one arm over his face as he came, and Tommy swallowed the rush of salty come. He gentled his touches, letting Felix slip from his mouth, and then moved up the bed to stretch out beside him.

He studied Felix silently. The cameraman's chest heaved and his arm covered his eyes, but his cheeks were flushed and a wild grin spread over his face. Tommy gently moved the arm and met Felix's blissed-out gaze with a grin of his own.

"That was fun, Pearce," he said, running a thumb over Felix's lower lip. "Thanks."

Felix laughed, a low rumble. "Any time, Nguyen."

Chapter Three

TOMMY CURLED up like a kitten on the bed and slept. Felix sat next to him and watched over him, resisting the urge to run his hands all over Tommy's body. He hadn't felt this close to another person in a long time. What a strange day. Tommy's light brown skin was covered in red marks, some bruises, some teeth marks. A few dark scratches. Most would fade before he woke up from his nap, but they looked good on Tommy's skin and they filled Felix with a tender sense of pride. Two days. They could have this for two days. Of course, they'd have to go back to being TV star and cameraman when they got to Maine.

Science Sunday covered the gamut of the sciences, but the Maine show was part of a special episode for an environmental science week, talking about climate change and the effects on aquaculture. Tommy had thrown himself into the research with his typical enthusiasm, and Felix was looking forward to seeing him at sea. They'd be taking a small local crew on a lobster fishing boat, with a second boat and a drone for the cinematography. Felix was the DP for this episode, a fact that filled him with anticipation. It would be *his* vision, *his* touch that showed in the final production.

Beside him, Tommy stretched and let out a soft noise. Felix glanced at him, and saw those dark brown eyes staring back at him.

"Hey." He smiled down at his bedmate.

"Hi. I fell asleep?" Tommy yawned.

"You did. How do you feel?"

Tommy stilled, then grinned. "Good. Really good."

Felix grinned back, then leaned over Tommy and kissed him gently. "I'm glad." He ran a fingertip over the bruise on Tommy's shoulder. "These?"

"Mmmm. Feels nice." Tommy stretched again. "Does that make me a masochist?"

Felix shrugged. "I don't know. Maybe. How do you feel about it?"

Tommy scowled, and Felix bit his lip to keep from laughing. "I don't know. Before this afternoon, if you'd told me I would get off on being bitten, I don't think I would have believed you, and yet, here we are, collecting evidence to the contrary."

Felix nodded his agreement. "Want to collect more evidence?"

A laugh bubbled up out of Tommy and he smiled up at Felix. "Yes. I think I do. For science, of course."

Felix lay down next to Tommy and kissed him again. "For science," he murmured against Tommy's lips.

They kissed slowly, letting the anticipation and heat grow until they were both hard and panting, and then Felix brought Tommy off with sharp bites to the thighs while Tommy stroked and played with his own cock.

When Tommy reached for Felix, he shook his head.

"Later. I like to delay gratification. Let's go walk around a bit and then get some dinner."

Tommy shrugged and eased off the bed. "If that's what you want. But I intend to have my dessert."

A rush of warmth swept over Felix as they got dressed. He wasn't sure what he would have expected Tommy to be like in bed, but he never in a million years would have expected him to be so sweetly accommodating, quick to smile and generous with his pleasure.

"Your ex was stupid to let you go," he blurted out, and Tommy paused, one leg in his jeans.

"No, he wasn't. But it's sweet of you to say so." Tommy offered him a bitter smile.

Asheville was a small city but one that was bursting with character. After a brief stroll, they found themselves watching a drum circle in a downtown park. Felix had never visited this part of the Carolinas before, and was surprised to find it populated by a curious blend of hippies and hillbillies, suited professionals and artist-types, some of each coming together for the drumming. When he remarked on that, Tommy just grinned.

"Hippies and hillbillies have more in common than you might think. This is the kind of place that nurtures counterculture. And Appalachia, regionally speaking, is distrustful of outsiders or anyone who might tell them what to do. Alden's parents—" Tommy paused. "Well, his dad was kind of a hippie type. A half-Jewish science teacher with a ponytail. And his mom is a good ol' country girl. They fit together somehow. And Alden is a nerdy queer atheist who likes spreadsheets more than people."

"How'd you meet?"

"College. We both went to Carolina. Grad school too."

Felix nodded. "Tale as old as higher education."

Tommy snickered. "So come on—what about you? Any great love in your life?"

Felix shook his head. "Nah. I mean, not really. Our shooting schedule isn't really conducive to dating. I had a guy once who I thought might be The One, whatever that actually might be, but it ended badly."

"Please tell me it wasn't because of our shooting schedule?" Tommy asked.

Felix shook his head. "No, he was *before*. After college, before I started working with you, I worked for CNN. He worked in the building. He was a deeply closeted self-hate case. He was also a cop."

Tommy side-eyed him. "Really? A cop? You dated a cop? In Georgia?"

Felix shrugged. "I know, I know. I was young. And stupid. And thought that just because we liked the same things in bed, we could work around our very different world views." He was almost embarrassed by how naive he had been back then. Fresh out of school, head turned by a handsome man in uniform.

Tommy was distinctly unimpressed. "And how did that work out for you?"

Felix laughed. "Obviously, it didn't." He wasn't bitter about that time in his life, but he didn't look back on it with any kind of fond remembrance either. "I think he's married now."

"I'm not in the closet because I hate myself, you know." Tommy said. "But this job—it's more than a job to me. I developed this show myself. It's my whole life."

Felix took Tommy's elbow and squeezed it. "I know. I told you earlier, I don't judge you for that. Even though I think the kind of people who would be mad about their kids learning science from a gay man would probably be mad about their kids learning science anyway."

Tommy smiled at him, one of his real smiles. "I never thought about it like that. I judge myself sometimes. My mom wants to see me happily coupled off. I wish I could give her that. I feel selfish that I haven't."

"It's not your responsibility to be in a relationship to make your mom happy." Felix squeezed Tommy's arm again then let go. "But I get it. Should we keep walking?"

Tommy shook his head. "Let's watch the drummers some more."

When Tommy grew tired of the drummers, they wandered through small boutiques and art galleries, then stopped to watch a handful of climbers scaling a climbing wall on the side of a building.

"Wow." Tommy's eyes widened. "You ever do anything like that?"

Felix shook his head. "No, but I'd like to try it sometime. How about you?"

"Same. Maybe we can work it into a show."

"You really will do anything for that show, won't you?"

"Like I said, it's my whole life."

"I'm glad I get to be a part of it." Felix's own candor surprised him.

"I'm glad too." Tommy grinned at him. "You make me look good. And you're good company. Of all the camera guys I've worked with, you're the only one I've specifically requested."

Felix stopped, stunned.

"You requested me? When?"

"All the time. For all the traveling assignments. I like going places with you. You're easy to be around. And since you never complained about traveling so much, you pretty much became my right hand. I thought you knew I asked for you."

All this time, Tommy had wanted his company too?

Felix felt a grin spreading across his face. "I'm glad you did. I like going places with you, too."

Their wanderings eventually led them to a delicious dinner at a small brewpub where they lingered over beer and easy conversation until Tommy looked at Felix and raised an eyebrow.

"Let's go back to the hotel."

Felix's blood heated at the suggestion. There was no doubt in his mind what would happen when they got back to the hotel room—and he wanted it more than he wanted his next breath.

"I'll get a Lyft."

They were quiet in the car back to the hotel, but Tommy's hand rested on Felix's thigh, caressing him with tiny, feather-soft touches. When they finally arrived in the hotel room, Tommy grabbed him around the waist and pulled him in for a kiss.

They ground together as their mouths tangled, and Felix moaned desperately—he hadn't been lying about enjoying delayed gratification, but every moment of the afternoon had heightened his awareness and appreciation of the man in his arms. He tilted Tommy's head to the side, biting at the long line of Tommy's elegant throat, careful not to leave any marks, but unable to resist teasing those aroused shivers out of Tommy.

"That feels so good," Tommy whispered. "More."

"Greedy," Felix whispered back with a smile.

"Can't help it," Tommy tugged Felix's jacket off, then got to work on his shirt, lifting it up, up and over his head. "Never felt this good before."

The words stopped Felix in his tracks. "Tommy."

"I said what I said." Tommy was pulling his own shirt over his head. "Don't make a thing of it."

Felix's eyes closed. The last thing he wanted was to put Tommy on the defensive. "Let's get in bed."

Tommy practically dragged him there, working Felix's belt out of it's loops and sinking to his knees. Felix gasped as Tommy's mouth closed around him, heat and wetness surrounding him, that mobile tongue sliding over the most sensitive part of his body.

"You like doing that, don't you?" he asked.

Tommy nodded around his mouthful, then swallowed.

Felix gasped and gripped his cock low, right above his balls. He was going to come, and he wasn't anywhere near ready. "Slow down, sweetheart."

Tommy pulled off with a long, slow lick. "More of that delayed gratification you like so much?"

Felix grinned. "Yeah, something like that. I want to kiss you some more. Everywhere."

They stretched out together on the bed and shed the rest of their clothes. Tommy didn't seem to mind being redirected—and he had the most charming habit of reaching his arms over head when Felix started nipping and biting at his chest. Did he know how sexy that looked?

Felix nuzzled his face into Tommy's underarm, then nibbled up the inside of his arm to his elbow and lavished it with quick, sharp bites. Tommy's hips were rocking up now, humping the air.

"Roll over," Felix murmured, and Tommy did without any hesitation. And oh, the back side of him was lovely. From the nape of his neck to the curve of his buttocks, his skin was smooth and inviting. His legs were covered with fine black hair, and even his feet were pretty. "I don't know where I want to kiss first."

Tommy laughed. "Everywhere. But I feel like you're doing all the work."

"All the play," Felix corrected. "This is fun, not work. Are you enjoying yourself?"

"You know I am," Tommy answered.

"Then don't worry about me." He slid his hands down Tommy's back to scratch at the dimples on either side of his spine above his ass.

Tommy wriggled and let out a delighted sigh. "So good. Do you want to fuck me?"

Felix closed his eyes against the rush of arousal at Tommy's words. "Do you want that?"

"Mmm, yes please." Tommy nodded enthusiastically. "Want to feel you bite me while you're inside me."

Felix scratched down the back of Tommy's thighs and Tommy jerked, then settled back onto the bed.

"How does this feel like so much?"

Felix grinned and bit the round curve of Tommy's buttock. "Do you have supplies?"

Tommy rolled over, groaning. "Dammit. I don't. Do you?"

Felix shook his head. "That's okay. It'll keep. We have all day tomorrow. If you still want to, we'll get some."

Before Tommy could protest, Felix stopped his mouth with a kiss and gave him a bruising pinch to the nipple at the same time. The moment the tension seeped back out of Tommy, his arms went overhead again. Felix took the hint and pinned them down with one hand.

"Ohhh," Tommy breathed, shuddering. "That's nice."

"You have a bit of a subby streak, don't you?" Felix didn't wait for an answer, instead moving his attention down Tommy's body to suck on one brown nipple and scrape the other with his fingernails.

Tommy laughed. "Don't know about that. Just know I like what you do to me."

"Fair enough." Felix took the tip of Tommy's cock into

his mouth. Tommy's hands jerked free and buried themselves in Felix's hair. Okay, not so subby. He let Tommy push his head down and thrust into his throat, then rewarded him with a rough squeeze on his buttocks.

"Fuck, Felix."

His name on Tommy's lips did something to Felix's insides. He took Tommy deeper, struggling to fit him all even though he breathed through his nose. Tommy thrust again, then gave him a warning tug on his hair.

"Gonna come," he told Felix sharply. Felix pulled back to watch as he pumped Tommy's cock in one hand and scratched his thigh with the other.

Tommy's eyes rolled and his body jerked upward as he came in a spatter across his chest. No sooner had he slumped back to the bed and he was rolling to pounce on Felix, pushing him down and sucking his dick with the fervor of a zealot.

The pleasure sweeping over him was almost too much to bear. He came without warning, straight down Tommy's eager throat, and Tommy moaned with what sounded like excitement. For a long moment after his orgasm, Felix felt like he was floating. He was dimly aware of sliding out of Tommy's mouth, and of Tommy cuddling to his chest and kissing him all over.

"Jesus, Tommy," he whispered, hugging Tommy tight to his chest. "Your mouth."

Tommy laughed and kissed him again. "Yours first. Sorry if I was too pushy—"

"Stop. You aren't too anything. You're a fucking miracle."

Tommy's blissed-out chuckle echoed through the room. "No, that's you. I've come three times since this afternoon. I don't think I've come this many times in one day since— hell, maybe ever."

Preening, Felix sat up to look at the fresh marks on Tommy's skin. "I wish I could take a picture of you like this."

Tommy shrugged. "Go for it. As long as my dick is covered and you don't show anyone, I don't care. I trust you."

"Really?" Felix asked. "Are you sure?"

Tommy nodded and pulled the sheet up to cover himself from the waist down. "Take your souvenir photo. I get to keep the bruises. For a little while at least."

Felix grabbed his phone from the pocket of his jeans and snapped a quick photo. Tommy looked completely debauched with bruises and scratches on his skin and a languid smile on his lips.

"Lemme see," he demanded, and Felix handed over the phone and climbed into bed behind Tommy. Tommy's smile widened. "Yeah, you make me look good."

"Cocky bastard," Felix teased. "Here, one more. Sit up." He pulled Tommy up so he sat between Felix's legs, then put his chin on Tommy's shoulder. He took the phone and held it at arms reach to take a selfie. "Say bite me."

"Bite me." Tommy leaned back against Felix.

In the photograph, they were both grinning like fools.

"Oh my God." Tommy half turned and buried his face in Felix's neck, kissing and nuzzling. "Send that to me, please," he whispered into Felix's skin.

Felix did, listening for the vibration of Tommy's phone when the message came through, then he tumbled them back down to the bed. "It's still earlyish. Do you want to watch a movie or something?"

"Whatever you want," Tommy said. "I have to look over my notes for Maine again. There are a lot of facts to memorize for this one. But it won't bother me if you watch something while I do that."

And that's how Felix found himself spending the evening in bed with Tommy, watching Netflix on his laptop while Tommy's lips moved silently as he committed facts about aquaculture to memory. No, this trip wasn't turning out anything like he expected. But he didn't think it was one he'd ever forget.

TOMMY WOKE to the curious sensation of fingertips brushing his skin, the barest hint of fingernails stroking along the back of his shoulder. He was being stroked like a pampered pet and he *loved* it. Goosebumps erupted over his entire body, and he purred with delight.

"That's very, *very* nice," he mumbled, rolling to face his friend, his colleague, his...lover? Felix smiled and resumed his feather-light scratching. His fingers trailed along Tommy's collarbone, then his thumbnail scraped along Tommy's Adam's apple and down to circle a nipple. Tommy shivered and reached for Felix's waist to pull their hips together.

Felix settled against him with a contented sigh. His hard erection rubbed Tommy's own and they picked up a rhythm quickly.

"Very nice, indeed." Felix leaned forward and kissed Tommy gently, then lightly bit Tommy's lower lip. Tommy shuddered and gasped, and then they were *really* kissing. Hands were buried in hair and tongues slid against each other. Tommy arched his spine and dug his fingernails into Felix's scalp, rewarded with a low groan that turned him on even more.

"Can I?" Felix gasped against Tommy's lips. "More?"

Tommy nodded into the kiss and moved Felix's hand to his chest. Felix scratched his fingernails down Tommy's sternum, then slashed them harder across Tommy's belly. When Tommy moaned in response, Felix leaned forward and closed his teeth over Tommy's heart.

The pain was sharp and hard, and Tommy saw stars as endorphins swept through him. This was the hardest Felix had bitten him yet, and it took him by surprise, but a part of him thrilled to it.

"Wish you could bite all the way through me," he gasped, and Felix let go, growled, and bit him again over the same spot, sucking hard.

Their pelvises rocked faster against each other and Tommy reached down to stroke Felix's cock, which was hard and leaking against his own.

"Give me this gorgeous dick," he said, pumping it firmly.

Felix threw his head back and groaned. "Your mouth."

Tommy scrabbled down the bed and took Felix into his mouth, shoving himself down until he gagged. Felix thrust into him once, then pulled him off.

"Turn around; sit on my face."

Yes, please.

Tommy maneuvered his body so he was kneeling over Felix, then returned to feasting on Felix's cock. He sucked on the tip while he scratched at Felix's thighs with one hand and pumped his shaft with the other.

Then he felt Felix's tongue on his sac. Gentle—so gentle, it was hard to believe this was the same man—it swept from sac to hole and back again. Then his teeth scraped at Tommy's taint, and he cried out around his own mouthful. He began to roll Felix's balls in one hand while Felix speared his hole with his tongue.

Heat rose in him, the intimacy of Felix's touch almost too much to bear. Felix gripped him by the hips and teased his hole with teeth and tongue.

Tommy had to let go of Felix's cock because he couldn't focus on anything but Felix's assault on his ass. Another squeeze, then Felix trailed a fingertip closer.

"May I?" he stroked the fingertip across Tommy's hole and Tommy shuddered.

"Please, please, please *yes*."

Felix's fingertips breached him slowly, carefully, because they didn't have lube, until Tommy rocked back on his fingers and begged for more.

"Stroke yourself," Felix demanded.

Tommy grabbed his own dick and started pumping it, pleasure sweeping through his entire body. It felt like pressure building in his veins, and he gave himself over to it, mindless except for his need to come.

Felix pegged his prostate and bit his ass cheek, and Tommy lost it. He came, and came, and came—and he couldn't believe he could still ejaculate after how many times he'd come the night before—but it pulsed out of him, and he shouted and slumped over Felix.

Felix's hands slid away, and he was turning Tommy around and kissing his face, his throat, his chest, murmuring sweet words about how hot Tommy was and how good it was, and Tommy couldn't do anything for a long moment but catch his breath. Once he did, he kissed Felix hard, reaching between them to pump Felix's dick until Felix was thrusting into his hand and nipping at his shoulder.

"Bite me, hard," Tommy told him, and Felix did—it didn't feel as good as it did before orgasm, but it still sent a shiver through Tommy, and it was enough to send Felix over the edge, throwing one hand up to cover his face as he shook with the intensity of his orgasm.

Tommy drew Felix's hand down and kissed him again.

"So good, Felix. It's so good with you."

Felix opened his eyes and smiled. "You—you're amazing. I wish we had a month in this bed."

Tommy felt a flush creep up his face and he grinned. "Me too. But—" he glanced at his phone. "If we're going to fuck like that for two days, I need carbs. Let's go get some breakfast."

Chapter Four

ALL GOOD THINGS must come to an end, including the best two days Tommy had ever spent with another person. He rose early Wednesday morning and switched on the TV, flipping channels until he found a cooking show. Something cheerful and talky to have on in the background as they packed.

Felix sat up in bed, gloriously naked. "Nooooo." He scrubbed his hands over his face. "I don't want to go."

Tommy grinned. "You didn't want to come here in the first place."

"Of course not. I thought I'd be sitting in a hotel for two days while you had boring ex sex. But then——"

"But then." Tommy agreed wistfully. But then Felix Pearce had said *When I fuck, I leave marks.* And everything had changed. Tommy ran a hand over the most recent bruise Felix had sucked onto his chest, right above his nipple. He closed his eyes, remembering how Felix had made him squirm with delight into the wee hours of the night before.

"That look on your face," Felix said, his voice low and

rough. "It makes me want to drag you back into this bed and cover you with a dozen more of those."

Tommy groaned and then laughed. "Stop. We have a flight to catch."

In the end, Felix did drag him back to the bed for a few breathless kisses but reluctantly let him go when his own alarm rang. "We really do need to start packing."

By unspoken agreement, they packed away the intimacy along with their luggage, reverting to the bland camaraderie of coworkers. By the time their plane touched down in Bangor and they boarded the small craft that would carry them to the coast, it was like the whole interlude had been a dream—something remembered with hazy uncertainty and disbelief. But Tommy knew he could touch those bruises later and remember.

They took an Uber to the production studio owned by the local crew to check on their equipment and introduce themselves.

The crew was barebones—a sound tech and a second cameraman. The sound tech would drive the boat. Tommy watched as Felix went over his plans for when they went out on the water. "We'll have one camera on the lobster boat with Tommy—me. One drone for harbor shots—I'll operate that as we're heading out. The other camera will stay on the other boat and get wider shots of the fishing operation. Sound good?"

The other camera operator, a lanky older man named Jimmy, shook his head briefly. "We're supposed to get some weather tomorrow. We might have to postpone the shoot."

Tommy pulled out his phone and checked the weather app. "Only fifty percent chance of precipitation, all in the afternoon. We'll bring raincoats."

"A raincoat isn't much good in rough seas," Jimmy

cautioned. "There's your equipment to think of. Lobster boats are open."

"We'll make the call tomorrow," Felix interrupted. "If it takes an extra day, it takes an extra day. He's right, Tommy, we shouldn't risk the equipment."

Tommy hated the idea of extending their schedule. Once they got behind, it set everyone in post production back also. And they still had three more segments to shoot on other coastlines.

"We can do the interview shots with the fishermen first," Tommy said decisively. "Then we can split up. Jimmy can do the rest of the lobster boat footage and then you and I can do the rest of the footage, the monologuing, on the other boat with the harbor behind me. It'll go faster that way and maybe we can get back before the weather sets in." He looked at Jimmy. "Does that work for you?"

Jimmy nodded. "We can do that. I'll give you guys a ride to the bed and breakfast and get you settled in."

There were no hotels open this time of year on this rocky stretch of Maine coastline, but they had made arrangements with the owners of a small bed and breakfast to host them for the next few days. In separate rooms, of course. Tommy and Felix parted ways in the hallway with awkward smiles and an even more awkward wave.

Tommy stretched out on the bed and slipped his hand under his shirt. He found the bruise and pressed, waking up memories of the night before. He played with it, scraping his fingers over it and digging them in as his cock hardened. Five years of easy companionship—*friendship*—overturned in two days. But they'd discovered something so much more potent than anything Tommy had felt before—and he wanted more of it.

FELIX CLOSED the door to his room and slid down to the floor. His heartbeat echoed in his ears and he tried to calm his racing thoughts. *Tommy. Tommy. Tommy.*

Was Tommy thinking about him? Was this new yearning something they shared? Or was Felix the only one unable to put the last two days behind them?

He unlocked his phone and opened the photo gallery, staring at the picture of Tommy in his bed. Bruised, blissed-out, all taut abs and silky brown skin against the white sheets, the barest scruff of black stubble. That had disappeared this morning. For five years, Felix had always only seen Tommy smooth-shaven, but now he didn't believe he'd ever think of him without stubble. Stubble that would rub against the inside of his thighs as Tommy tormented him with teeth and tongue.

Was this going to be his life now? Pining for the companionship he'd had for two days, that they'd agreed was just passing time? The sex had been good—better than good, if he was going to be honest with himself—but there was more to his yearning than just wanting to get laid.

He scrolled to the next picture. Their faces pushed together, laughing. Laughing. In five years, Tommy's smiles and laughs had been rare, usually tinged with the jaded cynicism smart men deployed to hide their loneliness. But for two days, Felix had gotten to see him like this: laughing openly, freely, with genuine affection and enjoyment.

Would his ex have been able to make him smile like that?

It was a mean thought, a petty jealousy. He didn't own Tommy's smiles. No matter how much he wanted to.

His phone buzzed in his hand and he opened his text messages.

It was a photo. From Tommy. Across the hall, sprawled

on a four-poster bed with a floral bedspread, Tommy had taken a selfie with the neck of his shirt pulled down to expose a purplish bruise above his heart. His eyes were closed, his lower lip bitten. He looked beautiful and vulnerable and like something that belonged to Felix. Oh, hell. He opened his jeans and slid one hand inside, the thumb of his other hand flying across his screen.

Felix: hot

Tommy: I wish we'd told them to put us in the same room.

Felix: I thought we were going to behave now?

Tommy: I can't stop thinking about your mouth.

Oh God, they were doing this. They were really doing this.

Felix: Tommy.

Tommy: Felix.

Felix: do you ever dig your fingernails into your palm to take your mind off something you shouldn't be thinking about?

Tommy: Yeah, uh, that's never going to work again.

He thought of Tommy across the hall, could picture him now in that flowery room, jerking himself slowly, pressing on his bruises with the other hand, maybe even scratching himself.

Felix: then dig your fingernails into your palm and think about me sucking your dick.

Tommy: you're evil.

Felix: You started it.

Tommy: I'm going to think about you when I come. What are you doing?

Felix: I'm sitting against the door, and I was looking at the picture I took of you and thinking about how your stubble would feel against my thighs. How much you liked my dick in your mouth. How much you liked it when I bit your shoulder. What it sounded like when you came, every time. And I'm stroking myself while I text with you.

Tommy: why do you cover your face when you come?

Felix's breath was coming in harsh pants now, and he closed his eyes. He opened them again to send his confession across the hallway.

Felix: Because a part of me is scared to feel that much

He was going to come. He was going to come sitting on the floor with his dick in his hand. Alone.

Tommy: I'm coming over.

Not "I'm coming." But "I'm coming over."

Felix stood and tucked his hard cock away, then opened the door. Across the hallway, Tommy's door opened and he rushed through the six feet between them, pushed past Felix, and turned them both around, closing the door and pressing Felix back against it.

Their lips crashed together and Tommy's hand was in Felix's pants and his whole world was exploding.

Felix closed his eyes, gasping and turning his head away.

"Look at me," Tommy pleaded, and Felix opened his eyes. Tommy raised his own palm to his mouth and bit the heel of his hand.

Felix came. His cock jerked in Tommy's hand and spurted across his wrist. Tommy stared right at him, watching his face change as pleasure undid him. Watching him fall apart and pull back together.

Tommy's eyes closed and he bit his lip and moaned. "Fuck, Felix, I'm going to—"

Felix reached down and shoved his hand into Tommy's pants, barely having time to close it around Tommy's cock before Tommy was thrusting into it. He leaned forward, still shivery from his own orgasm, and bit Tommy's neck.

Tommy gasped when he came, holding Felix by the shoulders and fucking his hand in powerful thrusts.

They sank down to the floor, unable to hold each other up.

"What the fuck was that?" Felix asked, trying to catch his breath.

"Us utterly failing at keeping things profesh." Tommy snorted as he laughed. "And possibly defiling a two hundred year old door."

"Why?" Felix blurted.

Tommy shrugged and kissed him, a gentle, sweet kiss full of reassurance. "Because it feels good. And I don't think that's anything to be scared of."

Felix shook his head. "You really are something else, Tommy Nguyen."

Tommy reached up and touched the side of his neck. "Is this going to show on screen?"

Felix pushed Tommy's fingers away and touched the bite mark as he examined it. It was red, but it wasn't going to bruise. "No. It'll fade before tomorrow. I should have been more careful. Sorry."

Tommy closed his eyes. "I almost wish it were bruised. God, I am so tired of hiding."

A shiver ran through Felix. "Don't say that. The show is your whole life. This is just—" He stopped. Just what? He didn't have the words. Dammit.

"I know. I know. What I don't know is how we're supposed to go back to work and pretend like this didn't happen. How I'm supposed to know you're watching me through that camera and that you've seen me naked and you've left marks on my skin. I feel like everyone is going to see it on my face every time I look at you."

Felix sighed and threaded his fingers through Tommy's. "You're better at hiding your feelings than all that. No one will be able to tell. I *will* be on my best behavior. And so will you."

Tommy nodded. "I'll try."

"Let's start with sending you back to your own room to

get cleaned up. It's been a long day already—do you want to go get dinner?"

"Okay. I don't know if there are any restaurants out here in the sticks."

"As a matter of fact, according to Google, there is a Subway inside the gas station we passed on the way here. I looked it up while you were asking Jimmy about his wedding videography business."

"You are so practical. I love it. Okay. I'm going to go get cleaned up and then we can go get a couple of footlongs and some chips."

Felix watched Tommy cross the hallway and then closed the door and leaned his forehead against it. He still hadn't gotten more than three feet into the room.

Chapter Five

IT WAS STILL DARK when Jimmy picked them up in front of the bed and breakfast. They had insisted to the proprietors—Jackie and Evelyn, a lesbian couple in their seventies who had been slightly star struck to host a television personality—that they didn't need a full hot breakfast that early, but they were handed a warm paper bag anyway. There were fresh, hot bagels sandwiched around cream cheese and lox, hard boiled eggs, and two steaming Thermoses of coffee.

"And here." One of the women handed Tommy another, larger Thermos. "This is soup, for later. It gets cold out on the water. You Georgia boys will need warming up."

"You didn't need to do this." Tommy smiled at her. "But thank you."

"It's Campbells," The other woman answered. "But you're welcome."

As they climbed into Jimmy's truck, Tommy turned to Felix. "We need to send them a thank you note. That was really sweet."

"I think Evelyn had a crush on you," Felix teased.

"Which one was Evelyn?"

"*It's Campbells*," Felix intoned gruffly.

In the driver's seat, Jimmy laughed. "Evelyn hates everyone except Jackie, but Jackie loves everyone. If Evelyn likes you, you've got a pair of friends for life."

The thought warmed Tommy. He met a lot of people in his travels, and though those acquaintances weren't like the deep friendship he shared with Alden, or the easy camaraderie he enjoyed with Felix, they did make his job more pleasant, and he appreciated them. Especially when they came with warm bagels.

The sun was beginning to peek out over the horizon as they arrived at the marina. Tommy and Felix checked over the equipment carefully to make sure they had everything they needed. Jimmy and Scott passed around orange hip waders and raincoats big enough to fit over the heavy jackets they all wore. Tommy felt awkward in the layers of fishing gear, but he knew he'd be thankful for it once they were out on the ocean.

They were greeted at the boats by Rich and Sheila, a husband-and-wife fishing team. Sheila was a red-faced blonde with a boisterous laugh, and Rich was quieter, speaking mostly in monosyllables. Scott showed them how to wear their microphones and how to turn them off and on. "And Tommy's an old pro at this, so if you forget, just ask him. I'll be driving Jimmy on the other boat."

"There's not a lot of room on the boat for two extra people," Sheila said. "So you need to move out of the way when we tell you to, and mind us at all times."

"Yes, ma'am." Felix answered. "We can do the interview portion on our way out to where you collect the—" he glanced at her for the right word.

"Traps," she supplied. "It'll take us twenty minutes or so to get out there."

"I'll film you and Tommy talking and stay well out of your way. Hey, Jim?"

Jimmy looked up from his phone.

"Can you get some aerial footage with the drone?"

"You bet."

"We figured we would split off from you after the interviews were done. Jimmy would join you on board and get footage of you fishing, and Scott, Tommy, and I will do some expository footage on the other boat."

"What's expository?" Rich asked.

"Have you ever watched my show?" Tommy asked.

"My grandkids love it," he answered, and Tommy smiled at him.

"He means the part of the show where I'm looking into the camera and explaining stuff to the kids. Where lobsters live and why, how old they are, how long the season lasts, that kind of stuff."

"The 'isn't science cool?' part of the show?" Sheila laughed again.

Tommy laughed with her. "Exactly. And science is very cool."

"All right, let's get moving." Rich glanced anxiously out at the ocean. "We're supposed to get weather later."

Tommy looked at the sky—it was a little cloudy, but didn't seem too bad. Maybe they were just extra cautious.

The filming went smoothly, better than Tommy could have hoped. Sheila was a gregarious hostess who could explain what they were doing in a way that kids would find relatable. She answered Tommy's questions as if she were addressing a class of kindergarteners, all big smiles and friendly gestures. When they arrived at the traps, she demonstrated how they would pull them from the ocean and then return them. And then she switched off her mic.

"If you've gotten what you need, we have work to do," she said with a smile.

"I think we're good. We're going to switch places with Jimmy now. Thank you so much for hosting us, this has been really educational and the kids are going to love it."

"You're welcome, boys."

Boarding the other boat was easier said than done as the two boats rocked against each other. For a moment, Tommy had a vision of them tumbling off the side, but Felix just scrambled over and then held out a hand to help Tommy do the same. Jimmy, obviously accustomed to ocean life, hopped across with an effortless ease, pulled out his camera, and started shooting.

"Wow, he made that look easy," Tommy marveled to Felix.

"Sure, but he does this all the time. He says he's done weddings on boats."

Tommy shook his head. "Amazing. Okay, let's do this. Hey, Scott, do you want to mic me differently over here?"

"Nah, you sound good through the headphones. Let's do your thing."

They shed the waders but kept the heavy raincoats to help with the spray from the wind crossing the boat's wake.

It took three takes due to increasingly choppy waters, but they managed to get the expository footage done by noon. A full morning's work that would equal one fifteen-minute segment of an hour show. Tommy was pleased, and enjoying the crisp air on the boat.

"I almost wish we didn't have to meet back up with Sheila and them," he said wistfully as Felix packed up his cameras. "I'd love to see more of the coastline."

"As long as you aren't fishing without a license, there's

no reason you can't go exploring," Scott shrugged. "You're paying for the boat rental all day. We're supposed to get some weather, though."

Why did everyone keep saying that?

"Can you drive a boat?" he asked Felix, who raised an eyebrow.

"Sure. Used to go fishing with my uncles all the time."

"Might be nice to have some time to ourselves," Tommy suggested. "Maybe talk about what's been going on?"

Felix's face flushed. "Hey, Scott. Want to go back with Jimmy and leave us out here to play tourist?"

Scott looked over at the two of them, and Tommy felt a small thrill shoot through him. "If you guys don't mind. You just have to have the boat back at the marina by five."

They would get to be alone, in this beautiful slice of nature where it was too cold to tear each other's clothes off. Maybe they could talk about what they really wanted from each other.

They radioed over to the lobster boat that Scott would be joining them on the way back. Twenty minutes later, their gear carefully stowed on the lobster boat, they were alone.

"I suppose this is different from fishing in Georgia," Tommy said.

"It's definitely colder." Felix smiled. "And the sea is a little rougher today than what we'd typically go out in from Savannah. Can't beat the view here though." Felix looked over at Tommy and shrugged wistfully. "You really are a beautiful sight, Tommy Nguyen."

Tommy closed his eyes When he spoke, his voice was rough in his throat. "That's very sweet of you to say."

"So now that you have me out here, away from

listening ears, what did you want to talk about?" Felix prompted gently.

And Tommy was suddenly at a loss for words. He knew, intellectually, that they should stop fooling around. End it peacefully, like adults. There was too much risk of exposure, and it made the confines of the closet so much closer and more real than they'd felt during the arrangement he'd had with Alden.

But he didn't want to end it. He liked Felix—admired him, respected him. He enjoyed working with him, and kissing him brought Tommy more joy than he thought possible. If only there were a way to have it all.

"Maybe we don't talk yet," he suggested. "Maybe we just keep exploring."

Felix nodded, his Adam's apple bobbing in his throat like he was swallowing back words. "Okay. But we'll have to eventually. Until then, we're all alone. Why don't you come stand with me and keep me warm?"

Tommy grinned. "It's not like you can feel my body heat through all these layers." Still, he let Felix pull him close, his back to Felix's chest, and he snuggled into the wall of Felix's body as Felix reached around him to steer. In spite of the layers, he felt intimately sheltered, like the world and his closet were both very far away, and he was safe from any decisions they might have to make.

HEAVEN WAS Tommy Nguyen in his arms, Felix was sure about that. Maybe not in the same way as having him in his bed, but in a sweeter, more poignant way. Somehow the impossible had happened, and they were together in a way that wasn't about blowing off steam or killing time. This was a different kind of intimacy than sex.

They didn't talk as they explored, except to point out the beauty surrounding them, sharing the experience in a reverent silence.

"Look—" Tommy pointed at a pair of big black birds arching across the gray sky toward land. "They look like little dragons. Or dinosaurs."

Felix smiled at Tommy's whimsical streak. He secretly thought Tommy related to kids so well because he shared their sense of wonder and curiosity about the world around him. The more Tommy let down his guard, the more Felix became convinced that Tommy's dry cynicism was all an act.

"Cormorants," Felix named the birds. "Definitely related to dinosaurs."

Tommy sighed. "They're beautiful, aren't they? I wonder if their nesting ground is nearby?"

"We can go closer inland, check it out," Felix turned the boat toward shore.

"But we can't get too close," Tommy cautioned.

"No," Felix agreed. He glanced at the sky—when had it clouded over so much? "And maybe we should head back after we check it out. Those clouds are pretty menacing."

Tommy frowned, his eyebrows drawing together. "The weather everyone kept talking about?"

"I'm afraid so."

As they drew close to the coastline, the waves were getting rougher and Felix had to put more and more muscle into the wheel to keep them steady. The boat wasn't a large vessel, just the deck and a tiny cabin below. If they were home in Georgia, it would make for a perfect craft to take on a romantic journey, maybe up the coast to Hilton Head or even Charleston, or down to Florida. He could imagine exploring the entire coastline with Tommy, and the fantasy made him smile.

Maybe, if he hadn't been fantasizing about the relationship he wished they had, he could have prevented what happened next. But he was staring at the curve of Tommy's ear and thinking about how he'd love to trace it with his tongue, and then all of a sudden, the world seemed to shift on its axis.

The boat lurched to one side as a large wave battered them, and Felix panicked as he struggled to right it.

Tommy spilled out of Felix's arms and fell to the deck with a sharp cry, and started sliding toward the low side of the boat.

"Felix!" he shouted, and Felix reached out to grab his arm.

He missed and Tommy slid faster, eyes wide and panicked as he scrabbled for purchase. He made a last, desperate grab for the railing, and time seemed to slow as Felix shouted his name.

The boat righted. Tommy landed back on the deck with a loud thump and a cry of relief. And then a terrible screeching sound tore from underneath them and the boat lurched again, this time with a horrible thumping noise from the engine.

"Felix, what was that?" Tommy's voice shook.

Felix couldn't form the words around the dread that filled him. He slowed the engine to a stop. Finally he choked the words out. "We hit something. It felt like a rock."

"We did what?" Tommy sounded as panicked as Felix felt.

"We hit an obstacle. In the ocean. And there's a storm coming in. Tommy, I'm so sorry. Put on a life vest right now. Pass me one too."

"What do we do? Can we get to the shore? Can we radio for help?" Tommy passed him a vest, then pulled on his own and began to fasten the buckles with shaking fingers.

"I'm pretty sure we damaged one of the engines, but there are two so the most important thing is water—I have to check the bilges."

Tommy's hands froze. "Those pump out water. We're taking on water?"

"Hopefully not. Stay by the wheel."

Down below deck, Felix discovered that "hopefully" was too optimistic. They were taking on water faster than the bilge could pump, which meant a hole.

Please, God, no. This couldn't be happening. He grabbed the cushion off the small platform in the cabin and searched until he found the source, then shoved the cushion into the hole. It slowed the water significantly, but if they were going to stay afloat, he had to do better.

"Tommy!" He shouted. Tommy's head appeared in the opening leading up to the deck. So beautiful. So important. So vital. He couldn't let this happen to Tommy.

"Look in the cabinet where the life vests were. See if there's any kind of collision kit. Hopefully, because this is a rental, they'll have something."

Tommy's face disappeared, and then reappeared a moment later. "There was this." He held up the kit. "Do you know how to use it?"

Felix shook his head. "I've never needed to. There are instructions. I'll hold this cushion here. Can you read it?"

A few moments later, Tommy was coming toward him with the collision kit and a wary smile.

"Okay, love. I need you and your cushion out of the way. I've got it from here. Why don't you see if there's an extra emergency manual bilge or go up on deck and radio for help?"

Felix's heart swelled with an emotion that was gratitude, fear, and affection all at once. He trusted Tommy to patch the hole as well as he could. And the man was a miracle in a crisis.

Tommy stopped him before he could remove the cushion from the hole, pulling him close and pressing a quick kiss to his lips. "I'm not certain of a lot of things, but I know this isn't your fault. And we aren't going to die out here. Science is cool. And you and I have a lot more of it to tell the world about. Okay?"

Felix nodded, not trusting himself to say anything.

Once on the deck, he tried the radio. It was possible they were out of range, but it was worth a try. He had to try.

After several minutes, Tommy appeared, pale but lovely. "It's patched for now. Do you think the one engine can get us to shore?"

"We have to try." Felix handed him the radio. "Can you keep up the S.O.S.?"

Tommy nodded.

Felix steered them toward shore, considering what he knew about the shape of the boat's hull. It was already damaged. He just needed to find somewhere they could stop and dock it—hell, beach it if necessary.

His heart sank as they approached land. There were no buildings anywhere, and the shoreline was rocky and harsh. Not ideal for beaching.

"There." Tommy pointed. A small island, not big enough for habitation, off to their left. It would have to do.

Felix steered them toward the island and slipped between it and the shoreline. The beach was perfect, neither shallow nor steep. His heart lifted again.

Tommy kept calling for help as Felix slowly, gently eased the boat toward shore, slowed the engine, and landed them.

He turned toward Tommy, shaking all over. Tommy dropped the radio and opened his arms.

Felix moved into them, and they were hugging, and Tommy's lips were seeking his with fervent desperation. They kissed, hard and hungry, and then pulled apart.

"We're on dry land. When we don't show up by five o'clock, they'll start looking for us. You did it, Felix. You saved us."

"*You* saved us. You patched the hull."

"We saved each other." Tommy smiled, then let go of Felix. "I told you we weren't going to die out there."

"We might still freeze," Felix grumbled.

"I'll keep you warm. Besides, there are heaters on this thing. I think the studio is going to have some words for us about the insurance claim, but I'm not going to worry about how much fuel we burn."

Chapter Six

WITH THE HEATERS RUNNING, Tommy and Felix sheltered on the narrow platform in the cabin. It was probably supposed to be a bunk for one, but without its cushion, it was barely more than a hard place to perch. Felix went up to the deck and came back with two more life jackets, which he put down on the fiberglass.

"It's not as good as a cushion, but we'll be more comfortable sitting on these."

"Thank you." Tommy held out his hand and Felix squeezed it. "I think we should send out an S.O.S. every fifteen minutes."

Felix nodded. "Agreed. Hopefully someone will come in range and hear us. Tommy, I'm so—"

Tommy put his hand over Felix's mouth. Sweet, sweet man. "Do not apologize. You were distracted because I almost went overboard. You were worried about me. And I looked around and around while you were finding the hole in our hull, and I couldn't see whatever we hit. You didn't miss something that was visible. It was an accident, that's all."

He watched as Felix's Adam's apple bobbed in his throat. Finally, the other man nodded.

"Now, come hold me for fifteen minutes before we send out the next S.O.S."

Felix dragged Tommy into his arms and cuddled him close. "I've never been so scared in my life."

Tommy shivered. In spite of his bravado with the patch kit, he had also been terrified. The fear had made him indignant. All these years, he'd refused to let himself long for a partner. That he could find someone like Felix—and realize, after five years working together, that he'd had a partner all along? And they would only get three days together? It just wasn't fair. And he couldn't bear the thought of something happening to Felix. He covered Felix's hands with his own, rubbing them to stay warm. "I was too."

"I couldn't tell. You were so calm. Except—why did you tell me that science is cool? Out there?"

Tommy froze, then carefully threaded their fingers together. "Because when you're on a sinking boat and you tell someone you love them, they might think you're only saying it because you're on a sinking boat."

Felix inhaled sharply as he parsed Tommy's words. "They would think that, would they?"

Tommy nodded. "I think they would. And I wouldn't want there to be any confusion."

"Tommy, science *is* cool. And I love you too."

Tommy closed his eyes and swallowed because there was suddenly a lump in his throat and tears in his eyes. "It's only been three days."

"It's been five goddamned years." Felix laughed and squeezed him tighter. "Five years traveling with you. Keeping you company on airplanes and watching you explain the world to kids. Five years, Nguyen. And you requested me."

Yes. He had. Because he had liked Felix Pearce from the day they met. Because he trusted Felix to never make him look silly. Because Felix was careful and attentive. Because Felix made him smile. It *had* been five years. This new part—touches and kisses, bites and bruises, passion and play—that had all grown naturally from their friendship.

"So what are we going to do about it?" Tommy asked, turning around so he could face the man he loved.

Felix touched his face with one gentle finger. "We're going to send out another S.O.S. Because we're still ship-wrecked on an island off shore, with no food, and it's cold as polar bear balls."

"We have soup," Tommy said. "My girlfriends Evelyn and Jackie made it."

"It's Campbells," Felix deadpanned, then laughed and stood up. "I'm going up on deck to the radio. Stay warm down here."

"Wait." Tommy grabbed at his hand. "I love you, Felix."

Felix smiled. "Science is cool."

Tommy listened as Felix repeated their position over the radio. He was cold and hungry and exhausted, but he was alive and in love and exultant.

FELIX REPEATED his S.O.S for five minutes, then dug the Thermos of soup out of their supplies and set a timer on his watch to come back up again in fifteen.

"No joy?" Tommy asked when he returned to the cabin.

Felix shook his head and handed over the Thermos. He watched as Tommy took a swig of the soup, and his heart seemed to swell with that same feeling he'd had on the boat, when Tommy called him "love" and said "I've got it from here." Fear and gratitude and affection—or, more simply, love.

"This is good. It's potato soup. And it's still warm. Drink some." Tommy pulled Felix down to sit beside him and handed him the Thermos.

"Thanks." Felix took the Thermos. "Tell me about your family."

Tommy shrugged. "Not much to say. It's just me and my parents. Dad is a dentist. Mom volunteers at her church. I had a very middle class upbringing in a neighborhood in Charlotte with a few other Vietnamese families, and I made them all very proud by getting into Carolina with a scholarship."

"And you're out, to them?"

"Yes. Since college. Now tell me about yours."

"You've hardly told me anything!" Felix protested. "None of the important stuff anyway."

"Like what?"

"You know, the science is cool stuff. The stuff you love about them."

"Oh." Tommy looked pensive for a moment. "My dad is the funniest man I know. He's very coy with his jokes, teases them out in a way that you're hanging on every word by the time he gets to the punchline. But his jokes are smart and never mean. I was still scared to come out to him, but he took me so seriously, and he was so kind about it. He said that it was going to be a harder life for me, but he believed I was strong enough."

"And your mom?"

"Mom wants everyone around her to have everything

they need and does everything she can to make sure we know we're loved. She can make all my childhood favorites in her Instant Pot, but when I come to visit, she cooks oxtails on the stove overnight because she says she likes it when the house smells like food for me. She never called Alden my boyfriend, just 'that blond boy' until after he was shot, and then she spent a week at our apartment fussing over him and was furious with me when I broke up with him a few months later. It takes time for people to earn her trust, but once they do, she loves them with her whole heart. I have never doubted her love for me."

"She sounds wonderful."

"She *is* wonderful. Your turn."

Felix thought about how to describe his parents, because his childhood was so different from Tommy's.

"I grew up outside of Savannah, the kind of redneck kid who couldn't keep shoes on his feet or grass stains out of his clothes."

"I think that's all kids," Tommy said, so kindly it made Felix's chest hurt.

"Yeah. But we were wilder than most kids. I have three brothers and a sister. And more cousins than digits to count them on. We were always running, brawling, breaking shit. My dad was at his wits' end with me most of the time and decided I needed a hobby. He had an old Minolta camera and taught me to take pictures, and I took it really seriously —my sister and all the girl cousins wanted me to take headshots to launch their modeling careers."

"And it launched your career in TV instead."

Felix nodded. "Mom's a middle school teacher, so you know, basically a saint. She loves your show. Our show. And she can't cook at all. Like, at *all*. My dad did all the cooking when we were growing up. But she always helped with our homework, even though with five kids it took her forever. And yes, I'm out to the whole wild clan, and they've been teasing me for years about 'that cute scientist on TV' I had a crush on."

"I'd like to meet them."

Tommy was smiling, and it made Felix smile too. "You will. Because we're going to get off this rock, and we'll meet each other's families, and we'll figure out how to do this *and* do our show."

"I was thinking about what you said." Tommy's smile fell away and he stared out at the sea. "About how the people who wouldn't want their kids learning science from a gay man probably wouldn't want their kids learning science at all."

"I shouldn't have said that. I know how scary it is to have your livelihood depend on people not being homophobic."

"But here's the thing—I think we were both thinking about it wrong. Maybe I shouldn't be thinking about the parents or the studio or syndication or even myself."

Felix frowned. "But it's all of those things."

"No." Tommy shook his head. "What if it's not those things at all? Maybe there are kids out there who need to learn science from not just a gay man, but a Vietnamese American gay man? Maybe there's a little kid out there who needs to see queer people named Nguyen or Tran or Le on their TV? And maybe I wouldn't be scared now if *I* had seen people like me?"

For as long as Felix could remember, he'd seen gay men —on TV and in movies, in books and art and everywhere. But they all looked like himself, so he never considered that representation any more deeply than that.

"I'm sorry, I never thought about how that would feel. I should have." Felix wrapped an arm around Tommy. "Whatever you choose to do, I'll support you and love you, and be there on set to make you look good, and on airplanes to keep you company."

Tommy kissed him then, slow and sweet, cold fingers pressed to cold faces. When Felix's watch buzzed, Tommy pulled away and stood up. "My turn at the radio."

And so went the rest of the afternoon, and well into the night, trying learn everything about each other in fifteen-minute increments. After the sun went down, the temperature grew frigid, and they huddled together as close to the heater as they dared, reassuring each other that they would survive this, because the alternative was unthinkable.

"Maybe we should take turns sleeping," Tommy whispered around ten p.m.

"You go ahead." Felix kissed his forehead. "I don't think I can yet."

"Well if you're staying awake, so am I."

Tommy fell asleep shortly after midnight, his head pillowed on Felix's thigh and his hand curling around the muscles there. Felix brushed the hair back from Tommy's face and held his other hand until it was time to use the radio again.

TOMMY WOKE ALONE in the cabin, curled up on two smelly life jackets. He was confused, and disoriented, and so *cold*. But he heard voices. And then it all came back. The wave, the rock, the hole in the hull that he had patched with icy fingers. Felix loved him. *Felix.*

He made his way onto the deck, where the air was biting. Felix was talking into the radio, and for a moment, Tommy thought he was just repeating his S.O.S. But then someone answered him.

"Can you turn on the lights? Is there room on the island to set a flare?"

"Yes, I've turned our running lights on—we had everything but the heaters off to preserve power. There were no flares in storage."

"How are you doing for fuel—is the cabin warm enough?"

"Yes, sir. We've been able to keep the cabin above freezing with the heater."

"What about injuries—you said Mr. Nguyen was asleep? Has he lost blood or hit his head?"

He looked at Tommy and smiled widely. "Actually, Mr. Nguyen is awake now, both of us are uninjured, and I think he's glad to hear a voice that isn't mine."

Tommy wasn't sure why that struck him as funny, but he snickered and blew Felix a kiss.

"That's good news. The Coast Guard has deployed air rescue to the GPS coordinates you gave me. Can you stay on the radio until they tell me that they've spotted you?"

"Yes, sir, we can stay on the radio until we're spotted."

Air rescues are terrifying.

Tommy could gladly have lived his whole life not knowing what it would feel like when a burly coastie descended from the sky in the middle of the night, strapped him into a harness, and then told someone else to lift him into the sky. Somewhere between terror and gratitude and relief, he simply burst into tears and hated himself for it. On the helicopter, he was strapped into a seat, and bundled into a Mylar blanket while another coastie took his vitals.

It couldn't have been more than a few minutes before Felix was pushed into the seat next to him, but it felt like an eternity before he could grip Felix's hand in his own. And then they were soaring away, and his teeth were chattering, but he was with Felix and they were going home.

"You guys are all over the news," the burly coastie said. "Not every day we get to rescue a celebrity at sea. At least you got your boat to that island though—the ocean's cold tonight."

"I'm not a celebrity," Tommy said.

"Everyone in my house knows your name," the other coastie said, then in a campy imitation of Tommy's voice, "*Science Sunday* with Tommy Nguyen!"

Next to him, Felix giggled. "More of a pause between sci- and -ence, I think. Otherwise that's pretty good."

"Are you fucking kidding me?" Tommy asked. "I don't sound like that."

Felix's giggles turned into a guffaw. "You know who does the best impression of you?"

Tommy groaned. "I don't want to know, do I?"

"There's a barista at the Starbucks in the Embassy Suites at Centennial Olympic Park who has your inflection down perfectly. She is a wonder to behold."

"Oh my God, I can never go there again." Tommy covered his face but found himself laughing anyway, and then he couldn't *stop* laughing, and then he was crying again, and the coasties were handing him tissues, and Felix was smiling at him like he was the most beautiful, precious thing in the world.

Their rescuers were called away on another mission almost as soon as they landed, and Tommy realized he didn't even have a chance to learn their names.

"Don't worry, we can find out later," Felix said as they were brought into the Coast Guard station in Jonesport. "There will be reports."

What a fucking understatement. When the military got involved in anything, the amount of paperwork was staggering. Tommy and Felix did their best to provide a report on where they had struck the rock—or whatever it had been—that damaged their prop. Felix, by some miracle of quick thinking, had grabbed his backpack as Tommy was being lifted off the island, so they had their GPS logs. From the GPS logs, they were able to approximate the location of the obstacle.

Still, it was hours before the Guardsmen finally told them they could go, and it seemed to take forever to arrange transport to the Bayside Camp Bed and Breakfast. They arrived to four friendly faces: Jimmy and Scott, who good-naturedly teased them about losing the boat before hugging them fiercely, and Evelyn and Jackie. Their hostesses clucked and fussed over them before kicking out Jimmy and Scott and sending Tommy and Felix to bed.

They didn't bother going to separate rooms. Tommy figured if Evelyn and Jackie gossiped—which he didn't think they would—he would accept that. Being safe and warm with Felix was what he wanted and needed more than anything.

They stripped out of the clothes that smelled like the ocean and climbed into the antique claw foot tub, filled to the brim with hot, lavender-scented water. Tommy took up the wash cloth and scrubbed Felix's chest, reaching around him to get his back, nuzzling his face into the silky skin of Felix's neck.

"I was so scared, out there," he confessed, his voice quiet.

"Me too," Felix murmured, taking the cloth from his hands and returning the favor. "But we're safe now."

They fell silent then, and Tommy just held Felix, resting his head on Felix's sturdy shoulder, and soaked in the comfort of the warm water and the steadiness of Felix's heartbeat. He started to drift off to sleep, and Felix nudged him. "Let's get in bed."

"Mmm. So tired."

"Me too. Let's get some rest."

The bed was soft and warm, and Felix's arms were strong and comforting. Tommy fell asleep in seconds.

Chapter Seven

FELIX HAD NEVER BEEN HAPPIER in his life to land at
Hartsfield-Jackson Airport in Atlanta. He'd also never been
more uncertain. In the seat next to him, Tommy stared
straight ahead, knee bouncing with nerves. They hadn't
talked about what would happen next. Felix had just
trusted they would figure it out when they weren't in the
middle of a dramatic life-and-death situation. But they'd
basically both slept for twenty-four hours and then they'd
come home. And it wasn't like they could talk on an
airplane surrounded by other people. Still, he needed reassurance.

"Hey, Nguyen," he murmured.

Tommy's lips curled into a smile, but he didn't look
over at Felix. "What do you want, Pearce?"

"I was just wondering if you still think science is cool?"

Tommy closed his eyes and put his hand on Felix's
thigh. "Science is the coolest."

"Yeah. I think so too. I just didn't want there to be any
confusion."

As they got off the plane and started walking toward

ground transportation, Tommy surprised Felix by grabbing his hand and squeezing it tightly before dropping it again.

"Did you drive to the airport?" Tommy asked casually.

"No, I took an Uber."

"Same. Would you like to share an Uber—to my house?"

Felix's mouth went dry. He glanced at Tommy, who was smiling at him. "Um, yeah. I could do that. Are you—"

"Yes."

"Then let's go."

The Uber driver was a talker, and he recognized Tommy. "Coast Guard air rescue at night? Y'all were all *over* Twitter. Everyone was talking about it. What were y'all *doing* out there?"

"Looking for cormorants," Tommy said, as if that was a completely normal thing for two people to be doing on a chilly winter afternoon.

"And your boat sank? That's wild, brah."

Felix pursed his lips to keep from laughing.

"No, we were able to get it to dry land. We did have to patch a hole, though."

"That's wild," the driver repeated. "Hey, can I get your autograph?"

"Sure, I'd be happy to sign something for you once we stop."

"Are you going to do a show about your rescue? That would be so cool."

Tommy laughed, not a real laugh, but one of the charming fake laughs he deployed so he didn't hurt people's feelings. "I will definitely pitch the idea. Although with what's about to happen to our insurance premiums, I suspect they won't want me anywhere near a boat for a while."

"Oh, that's wild," the driver repeated again.

Finally, they pulled up outside a small, white brick-front ranch near the Beltline, and Tommy signed a piece of paper the driver found in his car console. They collected their small bags from his trunk and Tommy let them inside.

"This is your house?" Felix hoped he didn't sound too surprised. "It looks so——"

"Boring?" Tommy raised an eyebrow at him.

"No. Cute. Homey. I like it a lot."

"Oh, thanks." Tommy smiled. "I bought it a year ago and I haven't had a chance to do much decorating. Our travel schedule and all."

"Yeah." Felix was suddenly at a loss for words. "What I can see looks nice, though."

"Why don't I show you more?" Tommy locked the front door, set his keys down, and took Felix's hand. He led them through a living room, past a bathroom and a guest room, and through an open door at the end of the hall.

Felix had fantasized about being in Tommy Nguyen's bedroom for years—though he'd never gone so far as to picture what it would look like. Tommy's bedroom was painted white, and it was full of light and plants. His bed was unmade and piled high with pillows, and a pair of running shoes sat on the floor at the foot of it. It was bright and beautiful, and Felix felt instantly at home.

"I like this room," Felix murmured, pulling Tommy into his arms. "I'd like to spend a lot of time here, if that's okay with you."

Tommy turned and kissed him, at first tentatively, like he was asking a question, and then fiercely, like he had all the answers he needed. Their tongues tangled greedily, silky smooth. The bed drew them in like gravity, and they landed on it and rolled together.

"Can I take your shirt off?" Felix asked, breathless.

"Yes."

Felix pulled the shirt off slowly, making hard, bruising bites over Tommy's flat belly as he went. Red marks appeared in his path from navel to chest, and he kissed the fading marks from just a few days before. *His* marks. Seeing them on Tommy's skin filled Felix with pride and hunger together. He wanted to spend a lifetime covering Tommy with marks like these. Tommy moaned and buried his fingers in Felix's hair. Once Tommy's nipples were exposed, Felix licked and bit and scratched them until Tommy's hips were rocking up off the bed. How perfect was he? To not only take Felix's kink in stride, but also to open himself up to it with a hunger that matched Felix's own?

Finally, he had the shirt off over Tommy's head, and Tommy was wild-eyed and breathless. Before Tommy could demand that Felix remove his own shirt, Felix reached for the button on Tommy's jeans. "May I?"

Tommy smiled sweetly. "You may."

Grinning, Felix stripped away Tommy's jeans and underwear with the same slow care, kissing and biting and scratching every bit of Tommy's skin as he exposed it, and then worked his way back up. He paused to worship Tommy's thighs—God, he loved Tommy's thighs. So strong and sexy, with their light dusting of black hair, and a bruise where Felix had bit him earlier in the week. Finally, he pressed a single kiss to the head of Tommy's cock.

"Will you take your clothes off too, please?" Tommy asked.

Felix nodded. "Of course."

As Felix pulled his own shirt over his head, Tommy surprised him by saying, "I like the way you ask permission before taking my clothes off me. It's sexy."

Felix tossed his shirt aside and smiled. "I think having

your consent is sexy. Knowing you want me to do… things." There was something about the way Tommy explicitly told him 'yes' that amped up Felix's arousal. *Yes* was the sexiest word in the English language when he was in bed with Tommy.

"I can think of more things I want you to do. But your pants have to come off first."

An arrow of lust shot through Felix, and he squeezed the bulge in his jeans. "If they have to go…" He trailed off, then dropped them to the floor and stepped out of them.

Tommy smiled up at him, then rolled onto his stomach, glancing over his shoulder at Felix. "I *do* have supplies here."

Felix bit his lip and moaned, then climbed onto the bed and bit Tommy's beautiful round ass. When Tommy shivered, he did it again, and then again, leaving teeth marks in that light brown skin.

"Mmm." Tommy humped his bed, and it awed Felix to see him like this, so turned on he couldn't hold still.

He scratched Tommy's back with one hand in long, slow sweeps that were more about sensation than marks, and then he spread Tommy's cheeks and kissed between them, delving his tongue into Tommy until Tommy had the sheets fisted in both hands and was pleading with him for more.

"Where are your supplies?" Felix asked breathlessly. The nightstand didn't appear to have any drawers.

"Box—under the bed."

The box was small and made of carved wood, and Felix was charmed that Tommy stashed condoms and lube in something so pretty. He opened it to find those and more.

"Do you—?"

"Like to jerk off with a plug in my ass? Why do you ask?" Tommy smirked at him from the bed.

Felix took what he needed from the box and slid it back into its hiding place. *Later.* Oh man, were they going to have fun with that later.

He put the condom on first, then poured a generous amount of lube on his fingers. He carefully slid them along Tommy's hole, then slipped just the tip of his forefinger inside, testing to see how relaxed Tommy was.

"Yes, more." Tommy shoved himself back on that finger, lifting his hips off the bed and moving up onto his knees. He rocked back and forth, and Felix had to close his eyes for a moment because the sight of Tommy like this was too much, too arousing.

Finally, Felix opened his eyes, smiled, and pressed a kiss to the back of Tommy's neck, sliding further inside and adding another finger. Tommy wriggled and gasped, and then Felix bit him right where his shoulder met his neck.

Tommy came unglued. He moaned and writhed in response to Felix's bite, absolute perfection. Felix bit harder.

"Holy fuck, Felix, please just fuck me, I'm ready, I need you so much. Please, do it, please."

And how he could deny Tommy anything he needed? He pulled his fingers from Tommy's body and added lube to his cock, then bit the nape of Tommy's neck again. "Roll over, love."

Tommy rolled, pulling his knees to his heaving chest. Felix moved over him, guiding his cock to the entrance to Tommy's body. He met Tommy's gaze and Tommy nodded.

"You may," Tommy said, smiling. "Yes, you may. Fuck me, Felix."

Tommy's body was tight, but yielding, and the sharp

intake of breath he made as Felix breached him was the sexiest sound Felix had ever heard. He eased forward, drew back a little, and then kissed Tommy as he thrust all the way inside. Fully seated, he closed his eyes and lost himself in the sensation of Tommy's body surrounding him, Tommy's tongue sliding against his, Tommy in his arms like he meant to stay there forever. It was all he wanted.

Tommy let go of his knees and wrapped his arms around Felix's neck, kissing like they would die if they didn't, kissing like the world was ending and he needed Felix to know that he was adored. When Felix shifted to kissing and biting along his jaw, Tommy reached between them, chanting, "Yes, yes, yes, please, yes."

Felix drove into Tommy with a rhythm that made his blood sing. Pulling back to watch Tommy's hand shuttle over his cock, Felix scratched Tommy's chest, and gasped with awe as Tommy came, spurting between them in milky pulses.

"Oh, I love you. I love you, please, Felix, look at me, don't be scared, I love you."

Felix raised his gaze to Tommy's and saw the look of awe and adoration there, and he wanted to cover his face, wanted to hide from his pleasure but then Tommy whispered, "Bite me, I love you," and Felix shuddered and came. He cried out, his voice harsh in his own ears, but he didn't look away from Tommy as he shoved forward with one last, powerful thrust, emptying himself into Tommy's body.

He eased himself free with a wince, quickly dealt with the condom, and made his way back to the bed and Tommy's arms. Tommy's arms, Tommy's kisses, Tommy's words—sweet Jesus, he loved the way Tommy talked.

"I love you," he said, gathering Tommy close to his chest and kissing his forehead.

"I wish we could stay here forever and not have to face the rest of the world." Tommy's voice was troubled. "The studio is going to be pissy about the boat. And I'm not looking forward to the meeting I'm about to have with PR."

"The boat is insured—and it wasn't a total loss. The hull can be repaired and the prop replaced. Besides, I was the one driving it. And you've gotten more press in the last forty-eight hours than in the whole time I've been working on the show. PR is going to love you."

"That's not the meeting I'm worried about." Tommy frowned and sat up. "It would be irresponsible of me to come out without talking to PR. And I'm afraid if I talk to them first, I'll let someone talk me out of it, or they'll threaten the show, and the closet door will be locked tighter than ever."

"Would you like me to come with you?"

Tommy kissed him, sliding a hand into his hair, then settled back against his shoulder. "No. Thank you. But if you wanted to wait outside for me, I would really appreciate it."

"Tell PR what you told me. That there are queer kids out there who need to see a gay man named Nguyen on their television sets. If they can see how much it matters— they won't hold you back. They'll help you."

"You have so much faith in other people. Where does it come from?"

Felix smiled. "It comes from looking through my camera lens at this beautiful guy who explains the world to kids through science."

Tommy made a strangled noise in his throat, then laughed. "Oh, this is how it's going to be now, is it? You're going to completely disarm me every day until I actually start liking people again?"

Felix bit Tommy's ear lightly. "I'm the only one you have to like. But I suspect you like more people than you let on."

Tommy twisted in his arms and kissed him again. "I more than *like*. I love you."

"I love you, too."

Epilogue

"WE CAN FOCUS GROUP IT, of course." The woman from PR gestured carefully at Tommy. "There are magazines that would pay you for an exclusive. You're famous enough that it would be a big scoop."

Tommy slow blinked, then pinched his nose. "I don't want to focus group my coming out. I want to talk to the kids. It's what I'm good at. I explain the way the world works. They trust me."

Darren, an executive from the studio who Tommy had known for years, who sat next to Tommy for what—moral support?—nodded thoughtfully. "You've never made yourself the story before. But it's important to get this right. Not just for us. For you."

Swallowing thickly, Tommy nodded back. "We could talk about Maine."

Darren smiled. "You could. It's good TV."

The PR lady smiled. "It would be better to do it sooner, rather than later. While the rescue is still on everyone's mind. And you should probably talk to HR."

Tommy glanced up at her. "Human resources?"

"The relationship, with your cameraman. It's something they should be aware of. There aren't rules about it, per se. But they should know."

Tommy blew out a breath and stood, butterflies wriggling in his stomach. His skin felt hot all over in a flash. He was doing this. He was really doing this.

"Okay. We'll talk to HR. And I'll start working up an outline for the episode."

Darren stood and held out his hand. Tommy shook it and met Darren's gaze.

"I'm proud of you Tommy. This is a big deal, and we've got your back."

ON AN UNSEASONABLY WARM day in early March, *Science Sunday* did a special episode on the dramatic events of Tommy and Felix's trip to Maine.

Tommy barely shook at all as he looked into Felix's camera and explained how the cold temperatures and the rough seas made a rescue by boat difficult before he launched into an explanation of the physics behind helicopter flight.

Behind the camera, Felix watched as the man he loved made a demonstration about radio signals and GPS satellites, and all the elements that came together to make their dramatic helicopter rescue possible. And when Tommy looked right into the camera and said "Isn't science cool?" Felix heard, "I love you, I love you, I love you."

At the end of the episode, another cameraman stepped in, and Felix turned his camera off and joined Tommy on set.

Tommy smiled at him, then they both looked into the prompter. Felix wasn't used to being on this side of the camera, and nerves set his heart racing. For Tommy, he could do anything. He took a deep breath and waited for his cue.

"The most important part of what happened during our day out at sea was teamwork." Tommy began. "Just like I always tell you: science doesn't happen in a vacuum. Scientists have to work together. And so did my cameraman, Felix, and I when our boat hit that submerged obstacle at sea. Because Felix was able to think fast and slow the flood of water into our boat, I was able to get the repair kit and patch the hull. It's important to work together in emergencies."

Felix took over. "And because Tommy was able to patch the hull, we were able to navigate to dry land and keep ourselves warm until rescue could arrive. Teamwork saved the day."

Tommy continued, taking Felix's hand. "Felix is not just my cameraman. He's also my partner. I'm proud to tell you all that I'm gay, and that hosting this show as a gay man is one of the great joys of my life. Thanks to Felix, and to the US Coast Guard, and to Jackie and Evelyn from Bayside Camp Bed and Breakfast, and to Jimmy and Scott from Jones and White Productions, I'll have the privilege to keep teaching you about science. Isn't science cool?"

"Cut." The director's voice echoed through the room. "Tommy, let's watch that back and see if that's how you want it. Nice work."

Tommy squeezed Felix's hand and met his adoring gaze with a blush. "That's how I want it."

Felix squeezed back. "Science *is* cool."

Did you miss Alden & Kit's story?

READ ON FOR AN EXCERPT FROM THE REALITY
OF US.

Alden looked at the subject line of the new message in his inbox and took one long, slow blink before removing his glasses and pinching the bridge of his nose. Maybe, if he closed his eyes and counted to ten, the problem would go away. Like how unplugging his router and going for a Starbucks seemed to fix ninety-nine percent of his computer issues. He opened his eyes.

The message was still there.

Packing lists and partner assignments for team-building weekend

No. Just. No. Okay, so maybe he was in denial. Maybe he had really hoped that by ignoring this, it would go away. He knew he was the office freak, and he didn't want any part of team building, especially if it meant being paired off with someone who would chat his ear off the entire time they were hiking.

He blew out a breath and opened the email.

Flashlights. Spare batteries. Smartwool hiking socks. How could wool be smart? Hiking boots. Long underwear? In October? Dammit. He was going to have to go shopping. He looked at the calendar. He could totally still get two-day shipping, but he wouldn't be able to try any of this stuff on. And he *had* to try it on. Which meant—sporting goods stores. Alden's stomach rolled.

It's not that he had anything against fitness. He jogged at the park four days a week, rain or shine. He even did some crunches and pushups every once in a while. But he could order his running gear online and do his crunches naked on the bathroom floor while waiting for the water to warm up. He didn't have to go *out* to *places* where people knew stuff he didn't and then *ask them for help.*

A yellow banner popped up in the lower right corner of his screen.

New message from Kit Taylor. Open?

Goddamn it. Stupid fucker was probably hitting "reply-all" to express his boundless-fucking-enthusiasm for this macho survivalist bullshit.

Alden opened the message.

Hey partner, I'll get enough energy bars for both of us—I get a discount at the health food place next to my gym. Do you have any food allergies?

Glaring at his screen, Alden tried to make sense of the message. Realization hit him like a glass of icy water in the face. Kit Taylor was his assigned partner for the team-building weekend. Kit fucking Taylor.

Lots of people in the office annoyed Alden, but Kit Taylor was at the top of the list. It was bad enough the man was a walking advertisement for an outdoor living catalog, all brawny muscles and thermal henleys under plaid lumberjack shirts, or that he looked like an REI model, even though he was actually a field biologist. No, Kit Taylor was also the kind of guy who volunteered for tough assignments and showed up to team meetings in muddy hiking boots. The kind of guy who probably kept a stockpile of canned goods and artillery in his basement, just in case the apocalypse decided to roll up on him.

The kind of guy who made Alden feel both terrified and inadequate. And somewhere, in his stupid lizard brain, turned on. Kit had a way of looking at him during the weekly all staff meeting that set his blood humming in his ears. It was completely irrational. Alden didn't date. He didn't even hook up. Not unless he counted Tommy, but that would be even more pathetic than just admitting it: He was celibate, for better or for worse, and he was too fucked up to do anything about it.

But if he wasn't? If he actually could tolerate the idea of letting someone past his carefully erected walls? Kit Taylor, with his giant shoulders and his tight shirts and his catalog-model hair, could definitely get it.

Alden hated him for it.

Partners. For their weekend in the woods. He read Kit's email again. He grudgingly had to admit that it was really nice of Kit to ask about the allergies. And to offer to get the discounted energy bars.

No food allergies, he typed back. *Thanks for asking. Why don't I double up on batteries?*

There. Even. Ish. How much did energy bars even cost?

The yellow banner popped up again. Click.

Awesome. This is gonna be epic. I hope you're bringing your "A" game, cause we can totally beat the rest of the team to the summit.

He even typed like a walking macho cliche.

Alden didn't reply.

Also by Vanessa North

The Lake Lovelace Trilogy:

Double Up

Rough Road

Roller Girl

American Heavy Metal:

Hard Chrome

Flying Gold

Blueberry Boys

Summer Stock

The Dark Collector

Hostile Beauty

High and Tight

The Lonely Drop

The Short Strokes: Collected Stories

Reporting In

Rigged

A Song for Sweater-boy

The Reality of Us

Rose & Thorns/Vertical Smile

Off Limits

Out of Sync

9 7 9 8 8 1 3 8 5 1 6 5 0